MW01127324

MICHELENE'S LETTER

MICHELENE'S LETTER

A Novel

Sim Middleton

Dave - Thanks so much for your friendship and support - Sim

iUniverse, Inc.
New York   Bloomington   Shanghai

MICHELENE'S LETTER

Copyright © 2008 by Sim Middleton

All rights reserved. No part of this book may be used or reproduced by any means, graphic, electronic, or mechanical, including photocopying, recording, taping or by any information storage retrieval system without the written permission of the publisher except in the case of brief quotations embodied in critical articles and reviews.

iUniverse books may be ordered through booksellers or by contacting:

iUniverse
1663 Liberty Drive
Bloomington, IN 47403
www.iuniverse.com
1-800-Authors (1-800-288-4677)

Because of the dynamic nature of the Internet, any Web addresses or links contained in this book may have changed since publication and may no longer be valid.

Certain characters in this work are historical figures, and certain events portrayed did take place. However, this is a work of fiction. All of the other characters, names, and events as well as all places, incidents, organizations, and dialogue in this novel are either the products of the author's imagination or are used fictitiously.

ISBN: 978-0-595-45631-4 (pbk)
ISBN: 978-0-595-71234-2 (cloth)
ISBN: 978-0-595-89934-0 (ebk)

Printed in the United States of America

FOREWORD

Folks with long memories, who have spent a while in Price, Utah may recognize certain aspects of "Collier, Utah." Also, the little mining town of "Dragger" might seem a poorly disguised version of Dragerton, Utah, a bustling company town during WW II but now a sparsely populated community known as East Carbon, Utah.

These are indeed the models for the locales of our story but, I hasten to add, the people in the stories are but figments of the author's imaginings about long ago events and actors.

Please accept this as the required disclaimer against slander and libel of anyone who might think they recognize a real person herein.

Sim Middleton

Chapter 1

Phoenix, Arizona—1945

A cumulus-like haze of tobacco smoke formed against the high ceiling of a small hearing room in the old city hall. Captain Wayne Carleton squirmed uncomfortably in a too-tight suit. The chief of police, Joe Rawlins, rolled his cigar in his fingers, staring first at it then toward the window. The city attorney, Bill Fogerty, likewise seemed ill-at-ease. It was stuffy, Phoenix in the winter was still warm, and noisy, whirring fans notwithstanding, the men's shirt collars had lost whatever starch they may have had.

The Chief finally took a drag on the acrid stogie and looked at the Captain. "Guess we might as well get this over with, Wayne. We've looked at it every which way from Sunday and it comes down to the simple fact that there's no way to keep you on."

"Don't amount to a crime, maybe," said the city attorney, "but you can't shoot a citizen after being caught in bed with his wife and expect to stay on as a police captain; not after the trashing we all took in the papers." Fogerty took a cigarette from his vest pocket and lit it. "Anything else you want to say?"

Wayne ran a finger along his damp collar and loosened his tie. "No more than what I said already, I acted in self defense."

"Yeah, and that's all that saved us from having to prosecute you, but the circumstances don't give it that much weight. Just blind luck you only winged the son of a bitch." The chief gave Wayne a slit-eyed look and twirled the cigar in his mouth. "You're the last man on the department I'd a thought would end up like this Wayne, but here's the nut of it: turn in your badge and other department property Friday."

Pancho's, a thick-walled adobe road house near the Superstition Mountains on the way to Apache Junction had long been a watering-hole for drifters, cowboys and occasionally, lawmen. Its dark interior was cool and quiet. A couple of modest neon signs blinked above the bar advertising *Miller's High Life* and *Coors.* Wayne ordered another round of beers for himself and Bart Ramirez, a deputy sheriff and long-time friend.

"Any prospects?" Bart asked, lighting a cigarette.

"They're hiring up at Globe."

"Somehow I don't see you bein' a copper miner," Bart said. "You've been a lawman too long to go to work for a living."

"Maybe I should've stayed in the Marines," Wayne said softly. "When the war came I could've done some good, but Ruth wanted to put down roots. If she'd lived, of course, none of this would've happened."

"Well, count your lucky stars the husband was out on a limb when it came to the law. An honest citizen could a really had your head."

"An honest citizen wouldn't have set up his wife so he could murder her. He's lucky she wasn't hurt and that an incompetent investigation let him off."

"The strangest thing about it to me is she's gone back to him." Bart said, pulling a face.

The men finished their beers and walked outside into a warm evening, the western sky aflame in crimson and gold along the flat desert horizon.

"When am I gonna hear from you again, you think?"

"Hard to say, I heard about a job in Albuquerque. If that don't pan out I'll head for the coast and see what's available in the defense plants." Wayne gazed at the sunset a few seconds then shook hands with Bart. "I'll be in touch. Take care of yourself." He turned and walked across the dusty lot to his car parked in the shadows of a clump of yucca.

"Hello, Captain," a man's voice from somewhere near Wayne's Buick. Wayne made an automatic grab for his pistol before realizing he no longer wore it. He peered in the direction from which the voice seemed to come.

"Don't get excited, Captain."

"What do you want, Miller?" Wayne waited for the man to appear. "I'm not armed; you might as well show yourself."

"Now, that's mighty good, Captain, 'cause I got a message for you from Inez, whose life you ruined."

"What's the message?" The words had no more than left Wayne's mouth when a sharp blow to the back of his head turned everything black and sent him plummeting through an infinite, star-filled oblivion.

A blood-red blank filled his blurred sight and Wayne's thoughts would not coalesce. He lay on his stomach, face in the dirt, something heavy on his back keeping him from rising.

A voice: "Be still, Wayne. Don't try to move. I got an ambulance coming."
He lapsed into the darkness.

Lights, burning pain, head afire, Wayne's vision still blurred and all he could perceive were blinding lights and dim figures moving over, around him. The pain subsided, he felt himself falling again.

He awoke in a bed in a room gradually coming into focus, pale green walls and a window with Venetian blinds. A woman in white stood by the open door. "He's waking up."

"I always said you was hard-headed, Wayne, but when even a tire iron won't crack your skull that proves it." Bart Ramirez' voice.

"I've got one hell of a headache." Wayne scratched at the bandage around his head. "I don't see how he got behind me; he sounded like he was off to the side somewhere."

"Don't worry about it now." Bart stood to leave. "When you get outta here you owe me a steak dinner for finishing off the job you started ..."

"What do you mean?"

"I mean, last night, I shot that son of a bitch dead. Self defense, he came at me with the tire iron after he cold-cocked you."

"You shot him?"

"Want to hear something strange? Miller had taken his shoes off so he could sneak up on you; found 'em behind your car. He just didn't count on anyone else being around."

"Are you in trouble?"

"Not on your life. You're talking to the sheriff's office now pard, not some pussy-footing city cops." Bart lit a cigarette and blew a plume of smoke at the ceiling. "The sheriff understands how to deal with dangerous criminals. Be 'round to collect that steak in a day or so."

The small bungalow had been Wayne and Ruth's home in Phoenix since they moved there in 1929. They had just celebrated Paul's eighth birthday when Ruth gave her ultimatum: settle down in one place and stay there. Ruth being Ruth, Wayne left the Marines and took a job with the Phoenix police.

Ruth put the skills she'd developed making homes in Navy towns and embassy apartments from China to Nicaragua to work on the little house near the park in Phoenix. She made it her crowning achievement. Wayne and Paul were the focus of her life and she of theirs until the day she died. Now, the bungalow, virtually unchanged since her death in 1935, was like a museum to her memory.

When Inez came into Wayne's life a year ago she offered a healing touch for his loneliness, which had almost overcome him since Paul went off to the war. She made him realize the depth of his needs and aroused long dormant passions.

Inez was an exotic: beautiful, emotional and Mexican; a cabaret singer. He'd known from the start that getting involved with her was wrong. He'd met her during an investigation. She'd been a source of information though not directly involved. Still, although she was separated from her husband, he knew she had questionable associations; things his libido led him to dismiss as not that important. But they were important and by the time he realized it, he was too involved. She manipulated his needs as a man and his vulnerability to scandal as a police officer. She was playing another game with her husband, Harry Miller, a man far less stable and more dangerous.

Wayne sat in the kitchen, just home from the hospital. Everything had turned into a mush. He was glad Ruth couldn't see what he'd come to. How he'd managed to be so stupid amazed him and had alienated a good many folks who had been friends. His name had been splashed across the front pages of the newspapers making him out to be a fool, a crook or both depending on your point of view. Now, with Bart's shooting Harry Miller to death the newspapers had started the whole thing up again.

He looked at the framed photo of him, Ruth and Paul taken a dozen years ago. How he wished he could start over. Paul was in the Pacific now leading a Marine infantry platoon. Wayne worried every day he'd lose him too.

Bart Ramirez, true to his word, called demanding Wayne meet him downtown at the Aztec Hotel dining room for a steak dinner.

"You got a dinner coming, Bart," Wayne said when they met, "but did you have to pick the most expensive place in town?"

"Figured if I help you use up your money it'll get you back to work sooner," Bart replied studying the menu. "You gettin' over picking at yourself? You screwed up good but you're still here and have to account for yourself somehow."

"Well, it ain't the first time, just the worst." Wayne said. "Think you'd get smarter as you get older; don't seem to be working that way for me."

"Whatever way it works, don't start feelin' sorry for yourself. The worse the mistake, the less room there is for that sort of thing. So, what's next?"

"Well, next is to wait for the fuss over your solution to my problem to die down. My God, the whole thing was all over the front page again this morning."

"Take it easy, Wayne. It'll blow over in a couple of days. There's no question about the shooting being justified and without some controversy everyone will lose interest pretty quick."

"I hope so. So far, my prospects don't seem all that good. Who's gonna hire an ex-cop with all this in his past? They'd already heard about me in Albuquerque."

Bart grinned. "Don't forget there's a war on; bound to be someone somewhere desperate enough to take a chance on you."

"Thanks, Bart; you got a way of putting things that makes a fella feel real proud."

"Fact is I happen to know someone that needs your particular talents right now. He's a friend of my boss who's just been made sheriff up in Utah." Bart lit a cigarette and leaned back in his chair, "Seems he's home from the war and lookin' for a good undersheriff."

"I've never worked for a sheriff before, and I don't know anything about the law in Utah." Wayne said, giving Bart a doubtful look.

"Don't worry, Wayne. It'll be kid stuff for an old hand like you.

Chapter 2

Dragger, Utah—1945

Alan Steger's right ear stung something fierce from the ice ball Ralph Mooney smashed into it as they both entered the schoolhouse door. Ralph bolted down the hall and pushed through the cluster of students outside their sixth-grade classroom. He smirked at Alan from the safety of his desk.

"I'll get you," Alan mouthed at him, furious, blinking back tears, his ear ringing. He ached for revenge. He wanted to smash Ralph in the face, grab him by that thick neck and choke the daylights out of him. He'd get him right now if Mrs. Mahalik weren't watching.

Alan made his way to his own desk, rubbing his aching ear, brushing out bits of ice. The smell of damp woolens and pine oil filled the crowded room. Alan's chattering, red-cheeked classmates began settling at their desks amid diminishing turmoil. Outside, gusting snow rattled the window panes.

Alan took his seat, his thoughts turning to the prospect of snow forts and sledding after school. He looked across the classroom to the sandy-haired, freckle-faced head of his best friend, Two-Gun Oakley—so called for a pair of cap-pistols he'd once owned. "Pssssssssst." A deftly flicked spit-wad landed on Two-Gun's desk. Two-Gun looked back at Alan, bobbing his eyebrows in recognition.

Mrs. Mahalik clapped her hands. "Come to order, class."

A new girl stood beside the teacher.

Alan had never seen anyone like her. Thin and pretty with an olive complexion, she had short black hair and large dark eyes that shone with barely contained tears. She wore a gray sweater and plaid skirt. Black stockings covered her legs.

"Class, this is Michelene Villiers. She's here from Lyon, in France," the young teacher said, a little distracted by an anonymous, frog-like croak from the back of the room. "Michelene's country is still suffering from the war and she's come

6

to stay with her aunt and uncle for a while." Mrs. Mahalik offered an encouraging smile. "I'm sure all of you will make her feel welcome."

During recess, Mrs. Mahalik walked out into the snow-covered schoolyard with Michelene and Shirley McCann, a prissy, bespectacled girl generally considered the teacher's pet. The other girls came to say polite hellos when Mrs. Mahalik motioned them over to meet Michelene. The boys hung back a moment, then scattered.

"How 'bout that?" exclaimed Alan, wide-eyed, as he and Two-Gun hurried past. "All the way from France, that's thousands of miles."

"Y-yeah, why'd anyone wanna come all that way j-just to end up here in D-Dragger?" Two-Gun wondered aloud.

"Listen," Alan said, grabbing Two-Gun's sleeve pulling him close. "We gotta get Ralph. He smashed an ice ball right in my ear from behind this morning."

Alan spotted Ralph tossing snowballs with some other kids, but Mrs. Mahalik and another teacher were watching. His plan for him and Two-Gun to grab Ralph and pack his clothes with snow would have to wait. The last thing Alan wanted was to lose favor in Mrs. Mahalik's eyes. He'd nursed a silent, almost worshipful, crush on her and her beautiful "Pepsodent Smile" since the start of the school year.

Returning to class, Alan noticed Michelene standing alone by the doorway, the promised tears running down her cheeks. He felt a surge of sympathy, an impulse to stop and offer some kind of comfort. Instead, he averted his eyes and hurried past.

Michelene was absent the next day but returned the day after. She seemed composed but subdued. Alan tried to resist his growing interest in her. In the first place, he didn't like girls. This French girl should be ignored. His dad said they had no business bringing more foreigners here. His mother said if the war was nearly over, why were they sending some refugee to Utah?

Alan busied himself with his friends and schoolwork. He tried to avoid thinking about Michelene but her image, the expressions on her face, kept intruding. She spoke halting English in a soft, lyrical accent, and the sound of her voice fell like music on his ear. Giggles from the class when Michelene mispronounced words offended him, rallying his protective instincts. But shyness, and his confused feelings, left him mute.

He spent most of his free time with Two-Gun. Both wiry twelve-year-olds, they lived two doors apart on C Street in the small coal-mining town. Alan grudgingly allowed his brother Ben, three years his junior, to tag along occasionally. Two-Gun, who had four older sisters, found Ben's company more acceptable but age denoted status and eight-year-old Ben did not qualify for regular membership in Alan and Two-Gun's little pack.

One snowy afternoon a month after Michelene's arrival, she and her aunt, bundled against the cold, walked past Alan's snow fort on their way to the company store. Michelene saw him and offered a timid wave. He looked around and, seeing no one, waved back.

"Th-that Michelene?" Two-Gun asked, stepping from behind a nearby cedar tree.

"Huh, uh, who? Where?" Alan stammered, surprised.

"You know, the g-girl you j-just waved to," Two-Gun said adamantly. "You like her?"

"No! I was just wavin' her away so she wouldn't come over."

"Yeah, we don't want no g-girls around." Two-Gun made a face.

"Naw, no girls." Alan looked back at Michelene and her aunt, who were fading into the thickly falling snow.

Alan returned to his work of fashioning an arsenal for the fort, a neat pyramid of smooth, hard-packed snowballs. And to one side, a slightly larger rock-hard, rock-centered snowball constructed for a particular target: Ralph Mooney.

Ralph continued to evade Alan's vengeance for the ice-ball incident. It had festered in his mind so long he'd been pushed beyond the bounds of fair play. Alan was reduced to this, a rock-loaded snowball.

With an unerring eye, and using his thin body and long arms like a whip, Alan would not miss. Ralph would feel the pain he'd inflicted and then some. But again, Ralph failed to show and Alan used the rock-ball to fell a wood "No Sledding" sign near the library, thirty feet away.

The library was at the bottom of "suicide slope," a footpath most of the year which, in winter, became a challenging sled raceway winding down a steep hill behind the fire station through cedar trees and boulders.

"This is it, Two-Gun," Alan shouted, propping the rusty old Flexible Flyer in front of him at the top of the slope. "I'm goin' for the record."

"I got the r-record," Two-Gun replied. "You ain't got a chance."

"Fair count," Alan yelled taking a running start and belly-flopping on the sled. The trail began with a sharp, stomach-tumbling, forty-foot drop to a house-sized boulder where it veered left. Alan leaned into the turn, pulling hard on the steering bar, skidding and sliding to a quick right turn. Nine, ten, eleven ... he counted under his breath, trying to measure his time. Snow and slush flew as he sped around each twist and turn in the trail bumping over sudden drops, skimming barely submerged logs and rocks. Twenty-two, twenty-three ... he lost count watching for speed-blurred markers—a gnarled cedar, a fence post, the frog-shaped boulder. At the bottom, near the library, Alan spun into a snow-scattering sideways stop, jumped off the sled and yelled up the hill toward Two-Gun, "Thirty-two!"

"No siree! I c-counted th-th-thirty-five," Two-Gun called back from the starting point. "Fair count!" he yelled, with a running jump on his own rickety sled.

Alan watched and counted as Two-Gun and his speeding sled disappeared behind the house-sized boulder, re-appeared rounding the curve at the fence post, and went out of sight until he emerged again careening past the frog boulder.

Two-Gun skidded to a stop. "Th-th-thirty-one," he said, jumping up and taking a confrontational stance toward Alan.

"You're fulla beans," said Alan.

"W-we need a st-st-stop-watch."

"Or someone who can count better'n you."

By March, the snow began to disappear, reduced to brittle sheets under cedar trees and forlorn patches on the shady sides of things; soon replaced by mud and mire, mitigated by the anticipation of spring

Chapter 3

Michelene was still there, her English improving and the long silences of the early days getting shorter. She participated more in class and expressed herself with growing confidence.

"That's very good, Michelene," Mrs. Mahalik would say. "How many of us can say even one sentence in French?"

Her short black hair sparkled under the lights and her dark eyes glistened. The rare smile lit up her face—and Alan's heart. She no longer seemed so different to him. Rather, she was singular, unique in herself. What was it about her that commanded so much of his attention?

Sometimes, in idle moments, he'd imagine himself rescuing her from German soldiers who suddenly materialized from the cedars north of town. He fought savagely, blasting them with his dad's deer rifle. After he vanquished the Nazis, a small trickle of blood would run down his temple, just like in the war movies. Michelene would run to him and gratefully throw her arms around him, cooing tenderly.

Alan's imaginings never went any further. Just as when he had dreamed about saving Mrs. Mahalik from fates worse than death at the hands of the Germans and Japanese, so it was with Michelene. The idea of anything beyond winning her favor was too complicated to waste time on. He was content for now just to imagine being her hero.

Alan walked in his front door hungry, but the smells that usually emanated from the kitchen were missing. His mother, a plain, stout woman wearing a drab house dress, sat at the table with a newspaper in front of her, dabbing her eyes with a tissue.

"What's wrong, Mom?"

"President Roosevelt died," she said quietly. "Go bring in some coal and kindlin.'"

Roosevelt dead! Alan caught his breath. It seemed as though the president had been a member of his family, like some distant grandfather. The name had always been part of his life. The familiar voice on the radio, the jovial face in newspapers and newsreels, sometimes cursed, sometimes praised. Gone? What would this mean? A sob caught in his throat as he went out to the coal bin in the back yard to fill the bucket.

Sorrow spread over most of the town of Dragger where the president was second only to John L. Lewis, head of the United Mine Workers union, as a popular public figure. Mr. Aldred, the school principal, decided a day of mourning would be observed and authorized the students to wear black paper arm bands they made themselves. During the morning recess, Ralph Mooney ran up and tore the band from Michelene's arm.

"These are for Americans," he yelled. "He was our president, not yours!"

Shirley McCann tried to comfort Michelene, teary-eyed and on the verge of crying, then took her to tell Mrs. Mahalik. After recess, the teacher called Ralph to the front of the room and told the class what he had done.

"You all know that what Ralph did is wrong," she said, looking around the room. "One of the reasons we're in this dreadful war"—her voice quavered and tears came to her eyes—"is because bullies have denied people their rights." She paused for a moment then continued. "Michelene has as much right as any of us to show her respect for President Roosevelt. And no one has to if they don't want to. That's one way we show our freedom." Her gaze swept the room. "Now, Ralph is going to apologize to Michelene and see me later about writing an essay." During the teacher's comments the red-faced, bushy-headed miscreant stood in front of the class with his hands in his pockets, scowling at the floor.

"I'm sorry," he mumbled with a nod in Michelene's direction. Then he quickly took his seat.

Alan hadn't witnessed Ralph's offense against Michelene, but confronted him in the schoolyard at the noon break. The long frustrated revenge for the ice ball, still smoldering in the back of Alan's mind, added to his outrage.

"How come you did that to her?" he demanded.

"Cause she's a frog and my dad says frogs are cowards and traitors to their own country," Ralph replied.

"You take that back! You can't call her a frog."

"Oh yeah, says who? Say, you sweet on that little, uh, Frenchy? Wait'll the guys hear that one." His mouth twisted into a salacious grin.

"You better shut up!" Alan yelled, shoving Ralph backwards and down on the ground. Ralph was on his feet instantly, arms swinging. Fists flew, doing little damage until Mrs. Salcido saw them and intervened.

"Here, here, stop that this instant!" she commanded, grabbing each boy by an ear and leading them off toward their classroom. They were propelled along, stumbling and kicking, heads twisted, still glaring and snarling at each other.

"What's this all about?" Mrs. Mahalik asked when they were delivered to her classroom.

"Nuthin'," said Ralph.

"Don't know," muttered Alan, mortified at having aroused her disapproval.

"I'm not listening to a minute of this!" Mrs. Mahalik said, angrily shaking her head. "You can take a note to Mr. Aldred and see what he thinks about your fighting! I just won't have it!"

The boys walked to the principal's office and dutifully handed him the note. A small, neatly attired man with rimless glasses, Mr. Aldred kept himself very busy and had no patience for minor distractions.

"Fighting, huh? Anything you want to say to me about it?"

Alan and Ralph shook their heads.

"All right, bend over and grab the edge of my desk." The principal picked up a paddle about the length of a baseball bat and administered three swift whacks to each boy's bottom. Both emitted involuntary grunts but no other sounds as the stinging swats found their breath-sucking, teeth-clenching targets. And though their eyes filled with tears, neither cried.

"Settle your problems somewhere else next time," Mr. Aldred said as he carefully put away the paddle. "Now, get back to your class!"

Walking back down the hallway Ralph growled, "I'm gonna get you, you creep!"

"You and whose army, you big jerk!" Alan responded.

Additional punishment for Alan came in the form of dusting erasers. Ralph was sent to help the janitor clean out a coal bin. Mrs. Mahalik separated the boys in their chores to avoid further trouble. And, she knew her students well enough to guess which of the boys might be more at fault.

What she hadn't planned, but allowed anyway, was that Michelene also stayed late in the classroom for extra study on her English lesson.

Alan was keenly aware of Michelene's presence and worked feverishly trying to think of something to say to her if the opportunity arose. He'd gone through the usual comments on the weather, had searched fruitlessly for some topic of general but mutual interest and decided to settle for a friendly "hello" if they happened to get within speaking distance.

"Alan," Mrs. Mahalik said, "I'm going down the hall for a moment. If you finish before I return, you may leave."

"Yes ma'am, thank you." He grabbed up the last batch of erasers and took them to the window to finish up. When he returned to the blackboard, Michelene spoke up.

"Alan," she said in her musical, accented voice. "Could you help me with a word?"

A little thrill passed through him. "Uh, sure, I guess." He turned and walked over to her desk.

"This one," she said, pointing at the text book.

He moved over beside her and leaned down to see where she was pointing. Her very nearness was so distracting he could hardly concentrate on the page. Her hair even smelled nice. Finally, finding the word and clearing his throat he squeaked out, "S-sens, uh, sensitive, yeah, sensitive."

"And that means ... what?" She looked up at him with her large, dark eyes and the hint of a smile.

Alan thought he knew but the idea of being wrong at a time like this was unbearable. "Uh, well, Michelene, (*there, he'd said her name and that too caused a little thrill*) I think it would be better if we checked Mrs. Mahalik's dictionary. I want to make sure you learn it right, okay?"

She stood and went with him up to the teacher's desk where they opened the big dictionary. He paged through the book until he found the word.

"Here it is. Sensible, no sensitive, uh, well, there it is," Alan said.

Michelene read the definition to herself. "Thank you very much, Alan. It was very nice of you to help me."

Alan found himself in a familiar quandary: tongue-tied. He desperately wanted to say more but not a word came to mind. He stood there, trying to smile, or say something. Finally, Michelene went back to her seat and gave him a last smile before resuming her study.

Chapter 4

Collier, Utah 1945

Sadie Mercer, the sheriff's secretary, was a handsome woman, maybe in her late thirties, with auburn hair who wore a stylish, conservative cut dress. A looker, Wayne thought, and then caught himself. Not the time to be sizing up women. He looked around the office: fairly new, a WPA building built just before the war Wayne figured. The sheriff's office took up one end of the ground floor, the jail half of the second or top floor. Courts and county offices occupied the rest of the building.

"Sheriff Buffmier will see you now, Mr. Carleton," the secretary said. She offered a pretty smile and motioned toward the sheriff's office door.

Wayne was surprised to see a very young man, maybe still in his twenties, sitting behind the sheriff's desk. He stood, limped out around it as Wayne entered and extended a hand. Looks like a cowboy, Wayne thought wondering about the limp as they shook hands. Wayne could see and sense a certain worn quality in this young man, that he was serious and unpretentious. Maybe something in the war had aged him. Wayne decided he liked him.

"How are you, Mr. Carleton?"

"I'm fine thanks, Sheriff, and yourself?"

They took a moment to look at one another, both offering guarded smiles.

"Have a seat," the sheriff said, motioning to a chair in front of the desk and returning to his own. "Have a good trip from Phoenix?"

"Yes; drove up yesterday."

"I was real glad to hear about you from Sheriff Phelps. I'd told him about my problem and he seemed to think you'd be the answer. He told me about your troubles down there.

"I'll be glad to answer any questions you have." Wayne said, embarrassed, his skin growing warm around his collar.

"Well, I expect one time of that kind of thing would be enough for any man." The sheriff looked at Wayne for a long minute. "Let's get to the situation here. I'll tell you right out that my experience as a lawman is limited. I was a deputy here for about a year before the war." He paused, looked out the window, then back at Wayne. "I left here in forty-two to do some work for the government and just got back a few months ago. The county commissioners appointed me because they had problems with their other choices and I was handy. But I have a problem too. No experience running an office like this."

"There's a lot to keep track of, I'd imagine," Wayne said. "And supervising peace officers can be tricky. But I wonder if there aren't local folks who know more than I do about running things around here"

"There are," said the sheriff, "but they all want my job."

"Well, that could be a problem."

"Yes and there's also a lot of things going on with the mines, the unions and the county in general that both of us will have to learn about. The county and this office have grown a lot while I was away."

"Learning will be my first big job. I know about police department operations but the jail and civil things you have here are new to me."

"I'm told that you're a fast learner, Mr. Carleton."

"I do my best, and if you think I'll do for the job, you might as well call me Wayne."

"Good enough, Wayne." He got up and limped back to the door. "Sadie, would you bring me a swearing-in form?"

"Were you hurt in the war?" Wayne asked.

"No, that's a souvenir of my rodeo days."

Wayne walked out of the sheriff's office with a new badge and directions to a store where he could buy a gun and other equipment. As he left, he nodded to Sadie.

"Welcome to the sheriff's office, Mr. Carleton," she said, smiling.

"Thank you, ma'am, see you Monday."

Collier was a far cry from Phoenix and Wayne wondered how well he'd get along up here. Phoenix was a relatively big city. This wasn't a bad place, just small and cold, with snow still on the ground. Collier sat at the edge of a desert against high cliffs at the mouth of a canyon heading up into the mountains of the Wasatch Plateau. It had a certain rugged beauty once you looked at it.

Wayne left his car parked at the courthouse and walked up the main street past the New Cardiff Hotel, where he'd taken a room, then another block to the Shotfire Saloon. He went in and ordered a beer.

"Two-bits," said the bartender, setting a bottle of Coors in front of Wayne.

Wayne tossed a half-dollar on the bar. "Anything going on in town by way of passing time?"

The bartender, an elderly, bewhiskered man wearing a white apron looked at Wayne a minute before answering

"You a gamblin' man?"

"I enjoy cards once in a while."

"They have a dollar ante poker game that runs here in the evenings. Anyone can join in if there's room." The old man nodded toward a large table in the back of the room.

"That legal?"

"Don't know if it's legal or not, been going on for years."

"Speaking of legal," Wayne said casually, "I hear you have a new sheriff here."

The bartender gave him a quick glance then looked down at the glasses he was washing. "You mean Tex Buffmier? Well, new in a way I guess. He was a deputy here before. He's just back from doing something in the war."

"Oh, what?"

"Nobody knows. Story is he worked for that spy outfit, the OSS."

"Don't say," Wayne took a sip of his beer and sat silent for a minute or two. "Someone told me he was a pretty good sort."

"Reckon so, least far as that goes."

Wayne finished his beer then walked across the street to a café where he bought a newspaper and had lunch. Afterwards, he got his car and drove to the New Cardiff Hotel.

"I might be here as long as a week, maybe less." Wayne told the clerk. He returned to the hotel that evening with a new .44 caliber Smith & Wesson revolver and holster. He had supper in the hotel's restaurant. Later, from his room, he called Bart Ramirez in Phoenix.

"Got the job."

"I'd a been surprised if you didn't. What do you think of the place?"

"It kind of reminds me of Globe. Not bad, just cold."

"Well, when you get settled in, let me know. I hear there's good hunting and fishing in those parts."

"Okay, Bart, I'll do it. Thanks."

A few days later, Wayne found an apartment in town. He'd had his mail forwarded from Phoenix to Collier, general delivery. Now he collected it, rented a mail box and submitted new instructions. He thumbed through the bundle of accumulated letters: some bills, his final check from the City of Phoenix, one from the company handling the rental of his house there, some personal letters from Paul and one that stopped him where he stood.

He recognized the handwriting immediately. His first impulse was to throw in the trash can in the lobby. He'd expected to hear from Inez after Miller's death and was relieved when he didn't. Now, his sense of relief vanished. It had been addressed to his Phoenix house and then forwarded, postmarked over a week ago. Had she tried to call him? He had asked the police department and the few friends who knew, not to give out his new address. The last thing in the world he needed now, Wayne thought, was Inez back in his life.

It was as if his long nightmare had followed him in the form of her letter. What miserable potential did that envelope contain? She had held him in some inexplicable emotional bondage while he was seeing her. Even after all the misery and the destruction of his reputation, loss of his job and abandonment by friends, he had to resist a recurring desire to see her again. It was like fighting an addiction. The letter brought it all back and with it a determination to defy her allure and his weakness. He folded the letter and stuck in his jacket pocket. He'd decide later whether or not to read it.

Chapter 5

The war in Europe ended on May 8th with Germany's surrender. In celebration, Dragger's volunteer firemen careened through the narrow streets in the town's only fire truck, siren blaring, wheels scattering gravel everywhere. People came out in front of their little brown houses and cheered them. A few of the men produced guns of one kind or another, firing them wildly in the air.

That evening at supper Alan's dad, Tom Steger, a thin, somber man with a sour disposition, said, "The paper says they think the Japs'll give up too by the end of the year."

"Oh, lordy, I hope so!" exclaimed his mother. "Jack's been sent to the Pacific now and Mildred's just worried sick about him."

"Humph," his dad snorted, shaking his head. "I never worried much about Jack, him bein' an officer and all, but I'd sure like to get a full tank of gas again."

Alan was of two minds about peace. He'd dreamed of growing up to go fight in the war and become a hero. What if it ended? Would there be another one for him? War was bad, peace would be good; so the grownups said. But if the war ended, what would he have to look forward to? He had no intention of becoming a coal miner.

As the last weeks of school approached Alan's feelings for Michelene remained intense but restrained. He hadn't spoken to her since the day with the erasers except for an occasional shy hello in the hallway. Once, when he picked up and returned a pencil that fell from her notebook she rewarded him with a smile and a softly spoken "Merci," causing a strange, warm feeling to come over him. Now, he realized he wouldn't be seeing her every day when summer vacation arrived. With all the courage he could muster, he walked up to her in the hall one afternoon as school let out.

"Hi Michelene," Alan said, a little too loud. "What're you gonna do this summer?" The words tumbled out so rapidly that the sound of his own voice surprised him.

She looked a little surprised too, but smiled and said, "I may go home to my parents if it is possible."

"Oh yeah?" a sudden anxiety came over him. "We can't even go back to Texas on account of the war.," Then, wondering if he sounded selfish, he added, "I guess getting back to your own folks is a different kinda thing."

Michelene stood with her eyes cast downward and said, "This place is so different and I miss my parents so much. I pray for them every day."

Alan looked at the floor, his neck and face flushing hot and said, "Well, I, uh, we all sure would miss you a whole lot if you went away."

Michelene looked at him with her large, dark eyes shining and with a little smile said, "I would miss you also, Alan."

The next day, Michelene was gone. Mrs. Mahalik told the class that she was returning to her parents immediately and would not be able to complete the school year.

Alan was shocked. He had been rather pleased with himself at having finally talked with her and had lain awake that night imagining how he might spend some time with her during the summer. He no longer confronted Germans in his daydreams about Michelene. His thinking had progressed to considering things that might actually happen, at least in his mind. Bike rides with her had seemed possible; even a picnic. Now, there was an empty feeling in his chest and a sense of loss descended on him.

For several days, Alan felt a strange, deep sorrow that he knew was because of Michelene but he couldn't understand why it felt so bad. Somehow, the school, the town, his life, all seemed diminished by her absence. Other friends had moved away while he'd lived here. He had been sad to see them go too.

It was different this time. There were no other girls like Michelene. It wasn't like she was his girlfriend. He didn't even think he wanted a girlfriend, but he wanted Michelene to come back. Her desk, the places he usually saw her, now empty or occupied by others, became little shrines that transfixed his melancholy gaze. He continued to puzzle over his strange new feelings and wonder about her and why her uncle had sent her away.

Alan's dad often mentioned Michlene's uncle during his supper table talk about goings-on at the mine. Mr. DuBois was one of the superintendents who lived on Grassy Trail Drive, the only street in C Section that curved along the bluff above the creek and had two-story houses. All the other houses in Dragger were small, brown, nearly identical box-like structures along dusty look-alike streets with alphabet letter names and few other distinctions.

Mr. DuBois, actually from Canada, was called "Frenchy" by the miners who, while suspicious of all bosses, were especially wary of foreigners. According to Alan's dad, Mr. DuBois acted like a big shot and was not well liked.

Weeks passed and Alan no longer felt the intense pangs of loss that had first bedeviled him, but he continued to wonder about Michelene. Every time he walked past the DuBois home he slowed his pace and looked at the upper windows, wondering which had been her room and if she had ever looked out and seen him passing by. He considered stopping and asking about her but his intense shyness prevailed. Would he ever find out, he wondered, what happened to Michelene?

Chapter 6

Curly Mayo stirred in his bed, gradually waking to the rays of sunlight sifting through the curtains covering the window of his small room. His head ached, as it did most mornings. He reached for a pint bottle of whiskey and took a sip to loosen his tongue from the roof of his dry mouth. He'd kicked his covers off on the floor again, still fighting the suffocating horrors that visited him almost every night.

The booze helped, helped him sink past the dreams, past re-lived agonies of being trapped under tons of coal, past the constant aches in his bones. But it didn't keep him there. Morning, or some hour beyond it, always arrived. And with it came the reality of another day, eased into with a quick snort of the Irish, Mrs. Mullin's coffee and, if his stomach could face it, a decent breakfast.

"Mr. Mayo!" her voice, loud and shrill as a crow's; must be later than he thought. He fumbled around under a *Life Magazine* on his night stand to find the clock. Yep, almost eight-thirty, she should be rapping at the door any second. There, there's herself now.

"Mr. Mayo, time to get up. Yer breakfast is on the table."

Curly was short, middle-aged, with a round, ruddy face and slightly bulging eyes. Whatever vanity he may have had disappeared long ago. He shook out the pants he'd left on the floor and put them on along with the khaki shirt with his badge pinned on it. After slipping on his shoes, he stumbled down the hall to the bathroom.

Ten O'clock and Constable Curly Mayo buckled his gun belt just below his protruding belly. He walked out to his old '34 Ford coupe, climbed in and drove to the Dragger fire station's office where he logged himself "On Duty," fudging the time by an hour. Someone from the company would come by later and check his entries in the log: the property checks, complaints from folks who flagged him down or found him at one of his regular stops. Neither he nor hardly anyone else in Dragger had telephones.

Problems with dogs, drunks or kids were Curly's jurisdiction as "Town Constable," duly sworn by the Clerk of Castle County as a privately compensated peace officer for the state of Utah and the Kaiser Steel Company. Any serious crime was referred to the sheriff's deputy in the area who Curly did his best to avoid.

All in all, better than being pensioned off back to Bernadine and whosever kids those were in Little Rock. Today, he vowed to himself to skip the drink until after two O'clock in the afternoon.

First, though, he should go by Nick's and see if Tom, the day bartender, had anything to report. Nick's Saloon was the hot spot in Dragger, if such could be said of the only bar in town. He pulled up in front, parked the Ford and went inside. Cool, dark and sour smelling with an overlaying odor of stale tobacco smoke, a comforting spot for Curly. It made him feel a little more relaxed just knowing the place existed and that he was always welcome.

"Mornin' Tom, how's things?" Now, if Tom offers a drink I'll just thank him but refuse, Curly thought to himself.

"Well, Curly, see you made it through the night." Tom took a swipe at the shellacked pine bar top. "You were pretty damn tight when you left. Celebrating V E Day's one thing but you was going for the whole damn war."

"Oh yeah?" Curly had no recollection beyond a general sense that he had, indeed, been here last evening.

"Yeah, and Nick told me to give you a message." Tom leaned forward on one elbow and fixed a hard gaze on Curly. "You gotta quit gettin' so drunk here, number one, and number two, you gotta start payin' for your drinks if you're gonna have so many."

"Well, uh, I didn't know it was gettin' to be a problem," Curly said, embarrassed.

Tom gave him a cold look. "Don't you ever read the paper? They had a story that someone here in town found you passed out drunk in your car last week. Raised a stink with the mine and the county; you better watch yourself or you'll be dryin' out in the county lockup in Collier pretty soon."

"I'll worry about that, Tom. You just mind things here and say the word when I'm outta line. I can handle it."

"Okay, and Nick said you should earn your keep once in a while being a constable." Tom took another swipe at the bar. "Kids keep coming in the parkin' lot and stealin' all the empties the customers toss out before I can gather 'em up, and Nick don't like losing the deposit on 'em."

"You tell him I'll take care of it Tom."

Curly drove out of Nick's parking lot. He tried not to let the shame get a hold on him. He'd read the paper. "Town drunk with a badge," someone had called him. He'd just have to live it down. He would quit drinking one of these days. If he could just get past the aches that still bedeviled him from all those broken bones. And the damned suffocation dreams, soon as they quit coming every night; well, pretty soon, it all has to get better.

Chapter 7

Summer vacation arrived at last. Alan and Two-Gun, seldom far apart, looked forward to the small adventures that boys with little more than time on their hands could find. They met as early in the mornings as mothers and chores would allow.

"You wanna ride down to the White Elephant today?" Alan asked as they made some minor repairs on their old, dilapidated bikes.

"Guess so," replied a somewhat subdued Two-Gun, moving a bit slower than usual.

"What's the matter with you?"

"Got a wh-whippin'."

"Oh." Alan studied the master link on his bike chain.

Reassembling the bikes, they took off. Their route led them past Nick's Saloon, where they made a quick pass through the parking lot looking for empty Coor's beer bottles, worth a penny each at Menotti's Market. Finding none, they rode on down across the creek and up the hill to town. Just past the company store, they took the highway to the turn-off for the mine, crossed the railroad tracks and followed the road through a cedar forest to the rim of the plateau on which Dragger stood. There the road began a steep, half-mile descent, known locally as the dugway, cut in the side of a sheer cliff to the desert below.

From the top, the boys looked to the southwest at the upper reaches of the San Raphael Desert fading away in the distance; a vast, splotchy-red expanse of sage, cedar, fantastic rock formations and sand. To the east stood the palisades of the Bookcliff Mountains, their dull ragged crags reminding Alan of odd-sized volumes stacked along a dusty shelf.

In Alan's imagination, fueled by voracious reading, mountains and desert weren't all that appeared before them. Besides the highway wending its way to the mine were a hundred vanished trails of yesterday. He could almost see the immigrant trains, their wagons and carts heading out toward Cedar City to hook up with the old Santa Fe Trail for the journey to California. And that plume of dust off in the distance, mightn't that be Butch Cassidy and the Hole in the Wall Gang ridin' hell-bent for Desolation Canyon in search of a hideout? No! By golly, that's a stagecoach being chased by a band of renegade Apaches up from Old Mexico.

"Two-Gun!" Alan yelled, drawing a gleaming imaginary saber, "Injun attack down yonder! Sound th' charge!"

Two-Gun gave his also imagined bugle a couple of spins as he swept it to his lips, "Tah daaaa, tah daaaa, ta da tada tada tada ..."

Waving his saber in wide arcs above his head, Alan leaned forward, "Chaaarrrge ..." and they were off, pedaling furiously, their two-wheeled steeds hurtling them down the dugway.

By midway down, the cavalry charge was over and the boys were caught up in the sheer excitement of speed.

"W-w-w-we must be doin' s-s-sixty!" exclaimed Two-Gun at the top of his voice.

"At least, maybe more!" yelled Alan, now noticing a high speed wobble in his front wheel as the wind streamed through his hair and the pavement blurred beneath him. Each bump and fissure in the roadway sent amplified shocks through the bikes' wheels and frames and the riders' bodies. The old, oft-repaired bikes, their patched tires and the boys' skills were all reaching their limits.

"Hang on, Two-Gun, here come the tracks!"

At the bottom of the dugway a rail spur from the coke ovens crossed the road as it turned south toward the mine. The speeding, almost out-of-control bikes hit the first rail with a jolt that pitched the riders up and apart from the bikes except at the handlebars, to which they clung with death-grips. The second rail immediately slammed them back together. The bikes bucked and careened, skidded and skittered as the boys fought to slow and control them. And somehow, braking, swerving and pedaling, they rode on.

"Yaaaay" Alan exulted, waving both arms in the air, "we made it!" He looked at Two-Gun, whose face was contorted in pain. "What's wrong?"

"I'm o-okay," Two-Gun replied, still grimacing. "I hit the cr-crossbars back there."

Half a mile on toward the mine they left the pavement and rode down a dusty, weed-choked lane, stopping at some long abandoned graves off to one side. The graves, dating from the previous century, were barely visible, the stones covering them having long since settled into slight overgrown depressions. The four larger, flat rocks that served as headstones had, like the inscriptions on them, become almost indistinct from the surroundings. A rock border, set by some latter-day passerby, marked their existence.

Climbing gingerly off his bike, Two-Gun said, "M-my mom says they were pr-probably pioneers who got sick and d-d-died on their way out here," opening their usual speculations about whose bones lay beneath their feet.

"Could'a been rustlers, strung up by a posse!" Alan said, wide-eyed, hoping for something more interesting. "Freddie Emery said their ghosts still howl out here at midnight 'cause this ain't consecrated ground."

"Ain't no such things as ghosts 'cept h-holy ones," Two-Gun replied looking morosely at the stones. "Besides, n-nobody would a gone to this much t-trouble for a bunch of d-drunken outlaws."

Alan picked up a small rock and sailed it across the road, hitting a tree knocking off loose bark. "Your dad still drinking?"

Two-Gun looked away for a minute staring mutely at the trees. "Y-yeah, and he b-beat up my mom, too. If I c-could get my hands on a g-g-gun I'd shoot him," he said, tears filling his eyes.

"You shouldn't talk like that Two-Gun, it's a sin."

"Yeah, w-well wh-what's this?" He turned and raised the back of his T-shirt, revealing several wide, red welts across his back. "R-razor strop, I got more on my butt and legs. Th-that a sin?"

"I don't know," Alan said, subdued. "It ain't right, that's for sure."

Another quarter mile took them to the remains of a large stone building known locally as the White Elephant. It had been erected about sixty years earlier as the station and office for a rail line from Collier, the county seat, to the original coal diggings near the present mine. Now, all that remained standing of what had been, for that time and place, a rather grand edifice of stone and concrete, was the crumbled walls. The rest had tumbled down into the basement creating an intriguing but dangerous jumble of rocks and chunks of concrete. Alan and Two-Gun, mindful of snakes and other critters, climbed down with long sticks and poked them into the gaps and holes.

Two-Gun clambered over a pile of rocks, jabbing gingerly with his stick at something in a crevice. "Bennie Hicks says the m-mine c-c-company use to keep its payroll in g-g-gold here and it ain't never been found!"

"Well, the Hickses practically started this place so they should know," replied Alan, peering under a slab.

"I think I h-hit some m-metal!" Two-Gun shouted.

"Reach in and see if you can grab hold of it!"

"No, y-you do it."

"Chicken!"

"I dare you!"

"I double dare you!"

"Well, I tr-tr-triple dare you!"

"I ain't scared 'cept what if your arm got stuck. You'd die of starvation or have to cut it off."

"Well, a-ain't no piece of m-metal worth an arm."

"Or starvin' over."

They got their bikes and headed home.

Chapter 8

The return trip meant having to ride their bikes back up the dugway, getting off to push the last hundred yards or so. It was nearly dark when Alan got home.

"I thought I told you to be back here before supper time!" his mother yelled from the kitchen. "And I want to know what kind of trouble you've got yourself into now!" She wiped a strand of hair from her scowling face with the back of her hand.

"What's wrong, Mom?"

"Mrs. Mahalik left a note for me at the post office to have you come see her at her house."

Alan could think of nothing from the school year that would be a problem now. His mother, however, was suspicious of anything out of the ordinary and sent him off the next morning in his best clothes with an all-purpose scolding for good measure.

Mrs. Mahalik lived on A Street, two blocks over and one down from Alan's home on C Street. Her house was identical to nearly every other house in town but to Alan it seemed nicer. There were potted plants on the porch and a store-bought door mat, small luxuries hardly known to most of the miners' families. She had the advantage, also rare among the miners, of having no children. Her husband away in the service, she shared her home with another young woman who worked in the office at school.

Alan approached her door and knocked, timidly at first and then, realizing he could hardly hear it himself, he knocked again. Mrs. Mahalik opened the door.

"Hello Alan, please come in," she said, smiling. She was wearing what looked like a man's shirt hanging out over slacks and had a scarf wrapped around her hair. Alan's crush on her, briefly displaced by his interest in Michelene, had revived. Seeing her dressed so informally sent an anxious buzz running up his back.

"My mom said you wanted me to come over," he said, staying on the porch, his head lowered and hands jammed in his pockets.

"I did, please come in," she repeated, "It's all right, I have something for you."

He stepped inside. The furnishings, though simple, were clean and had pretty feminine touches: pictures on the wall, a carpet and frilly lamp shades. Bing Crosby's soft croon drifted from a record player in a big radio console against one wall. So different from his home and others he'd been in, where some of the furniture was improvised Atlas Powder boxes and the rooms looked at once cluttered and barren.

Mrs. Mahalik, ignoring his nervousness, took him by the arm and led him into the kitchen.

"Would you like something to eat or drink?" She offered one of her beautiful smiles, like the women in Coca-Cola advertisements.

Without waiting for a reply, she produced a glass of milk and a saucer with two cookies on it. She set them on the table, pulled a chair back for him and quickly left the room. She returned with a piece of paper in her hand.

"I'm surprised at you Alan," she said. "I had no idea you and Michelene were such good friends."

Alan's face flushed hot. "I, Ah, uh, don't know ..." he stammered, his head again turned down, his eyes fixed on the edge of the table.

"Michelene sent me a letter from her new home in Montreal, and she enclosed one for you." Mrs. Mahalik smiled and pushed the folded paper toward him. "It seems that she's going to live in Canada. Her parents were able to emigrate, so I imagine things are much better for them now." She looked at him, waiting for a reply. "Don't you want to read the letter, see what she says?"

Alan held the folded letter in his hands, dumbstruck. He had almost recovered from mourning Michelene's departure, and now a jumble of confused feelings overcame him. Joyful that she had remembered him, he was embarrassed at having such a personal and private part of his life exposed. He opened the note and stared at the tiny, neatly written words without comprehension. Refolding it, he looked up at Mrs. Mahalik and in a voice edging on desperation, asked, "Could I please be excused?"

"Wouldn't you like some of the milk and cookies?"

As she spoke, Alan stood and moved away from the table. The teacher put her arm around his shoulders and guided him to the door.

"Goodbye, Alan. Let me hear from you sometime. I have Michelene's address if you'd like to write to her."

Chapter 9

Outside, Alan clutched the letter tightly, not daring to open it. He folded it carefully and tucked it into his back pocket. He wanted to read it but not at home. His mother might notice. She would want to know what was in it, and all about Michelene. He wasn't ready for anything like that. He looked around nervously, hoping no one he knew had seen him. Crossing between houses over to Grassy Trail Drive, Alan walked past the DuBois home, forgetting for the first time to look up at the second floor, and on down the hill to the creek. He ducked into the willow thicket growing along the creek bed where dark cave-like passages had been hollowed out. Alan made his way toward the center where a room of sorts served as a hideaway. Shafts of sunlight penetrated the upper branches, exposing the accumulated litter of other visitors. Alan took the letter from his pocket, anxiously anticipating Michelene's words.

"What'r you doin' here?" demanded Ralph Mooney, emerging from the darkness. Alan's enemy from school, crouching in the mottled shadows, looked more menacing than usual.

"Hey, Billy, guess who's here, pretty boy."

The hated nickname that even his friends sometimes teased him with, and worse, Billy Preston was here too.

Billy, Ralph's sixteen-year-old cousin, a surly, heavy-set boy, had spent time in a reform school in Kentucky and often carried a hunting knife.

"Pretty boy, huh?" Billy said with a smirk, looking out from the shadows, "Who're you, the town pansy?" He leered at Alan, "You a sister-boy, sweetie?"

"I said, whatcha' doin' here, creep!" Ralph demanded, scowling. "Hey, what's that you got there?" he added, pointing at the letter Alan still held in his hand.

"Nothing, none of your business!" He exchanged glares with the two boys, then turned and began to walk away.

"Hey, wait," Ralph said, "I wanna see what you got there!"

"I said none of your business. I gotta go!"

Alan had taken two steps when Ralph grabbed him from behind, clasped one arm around his neck and with the other, yanked the letter from Alan's hand. Ducking from Ralph's hold, Alan spun around, lunged for the letter, and missing, locked his arms around Ralph's waist sending them both crashing to the ground. Alan came up on top and swung a right at Ralph's head, landing it squarely on his left ear. He was seized by a fury unlike any he'd felt before. That letter was his sacred property and no one, especially not Ralph, was going to defile it. He pounded Ralph's head. "Give me that letter!"

"Go get it, rat!" Ralph crumpled the paper and tossed it aside. At that moment, Alan felt himself being lifted off Ralph and thrown to the ground where he landed hard on his back. This time Billy was on top and had his big, long-bladed hunting knife pointed at Alan's chest.

"You think you're tough, huh?" said Billy, a humorless smile on his puffy face. "I'm gonna show you tough, you little pansy!"

The blade's point pressed against Alan's shirt. He grabbed Billy's wrist with both hands and tried to push the knife away, but Billy was just too big and heavy. With his elbows against the ground, Alan held Billy's arm in place but could not push it back. Billy loomed over him, still smiling with a strange look in his eyes. He seemed to be using all his strength as he pushed on the blade at Alan's chest. Alan could feel the sharp tip of the knife moving closer, now touching him just above his rapidly beating heart. He thought of his mother and wondered if he'd ever go home again.

Both boys remained silent, Alan fighting to maintain his grip on Billy's wrist, a cold, choking fear rising in his throat. Can't let go ... can't let go ... can't let go, he repeated over and over to himself, trying desperately to forestall the panic he could feel crawling up his spine.

"Billy! Stop, you'll kill him!" Ralph cried out, finally breaking the silence. Billy ignored him, his eyes strangely cast, the little smile still playing across his moist lips. Another minute passed, the boys frozen in the deadly tableau, Alan hardly daring to breathe.

"We gotta go, Billy!" Ralph grabbed Billy's arm, shaking it. "We gotta go!" Ralph was screaming now, panicky.

And with that, Billy slowly began to disengage himself, got up and returned the knife to the sheath on his belt.

"I'm gonna let you go this time, you little creep," Billy said, "but don't rile me agin' or I'll finish the job." He turned and began making his way out of the thicket. Ralph trailed along behind him, glancing back, his eyes popping, scared.

Alan slowly got to his feet, heart pounding, gasping for breath, and began to look for his letter. He found a crumpled piece of paper where Ralph had apparently tossed it. He wondered briefly if Ralph had read it while Billy was holding him down, but it looked like he had just stepped on it. Alan brushed away some of the dirt and folded it over and over into a tiny square which he shoved deep into his pocket.

The sun was almost directly overhead when Alan emerged from the thicket. His mother would be expecting him home for lunch. He remembered wondering if he would ever be going home and was overcome at once with competing emotions of relief and terror as he realized just how dangerous his situation had been.

Tears welled up in his eyes and his breath caught in his throat. He couldn't cry. So complete was his humiliation that he couldn't imagine telling anyone what had happened. Besides, his mother would have a nervous fit.

He started for home wondering what lay ahead with Billy Preston and Ralph and wondering too, what Michelene had said in her letter and when he would find a time and place to read it.

Alan trudged up the hill from the creek past the squat, cinder block box of a building that was Nick's Saloon. He noticed the constable's car parked in front and paused for a moment, wondering if he should tell the constable about Billy attacking him. Mrs. Mahalik had told the class that crimes should be reported. But there was a bias against informers: Don't have nothin' to do with no law, his dad often said.

As Alan stood there, Constable Curly Mayo emerged from the saloon, blinking in the sunlight and pulling at the brim of his shapeless fedora. It was obvious, even to Alan that Curly had been drinking and was a little unsteady on his feet. Alan turned to continue on his way when Curly called out:

"Hey, you, kid! Come're! I wanna talk to you!"

Alan stopped and faced back to toward the constable. "Yessir?"

"You git over here to me right now!" Curly demanded, and patting his holster, added, "Don't make me hafta use thish!"

Alan shuffled slowly forward as Curly, weaving slightly, moved toward him.

"Now, you lissen to me and you tell yer buddies what I say," Curly said loudly. "Shorty here is sick and tired of you kids stealin' bottles off his property an' he wants it stopped! Ya unnerstan' that?"

"Yessir," Alan replied, again stifling an urge to cry.

"Awright then. You git outta here and you stay out, an' you tell yer buddies the same thing, an' you tell 'em I'll haul 'em into Collier if I catch 'em at it agin.' You got it?"

"Yessir."

"Okay, now git!"

Chapter 10

"What in the world happened to your clothes?" demanded Alan's mother. "You have to wear them to Sunday school tomorrow. Good Lord, what am I going to do with you? Every time I look you've made another mess for me!" She grabbed him by the shirt and spun him around. "You got in another fight, didn't you?"

"It wasn't my fault, Mom," Alan replied, tears suddenly flooding his eyes and running down his cheeks.

"Well," said his mother, softening a bit, "you dry up and get out of those clothes so I can see what can be done about 'em, and when you get changed you can have some lunch." As she turned to go back into the kitchen, she added, "And I want to know what Mrs. Mahalik wanted with you."

By now, Alan was really crying, although, except for the tears and an inability to talk, he kept it as subdued as he could. He went to his bedroom and removed the soiled shirt and pants and put on his jeans and a t-shirt, then sat on the bed, trying to regain his composure.

"What's wrong with you?" Ben asked as he came in and saw his brother. "You get a whippin' or something?"

"None of your business!" Alan responded angrily, trying to hide his tears. "What'r you doing here anyhow? Go on, get outta here!"

"I don't have to, it's my room too," Ben said. But seeing Alan's distress he abandoned the argument and after a decent delay to show that he didn't have to leave, he left.

Alan curled up on the bed. Everything was going wrong. But still, Michelene had written—at that moment he remembered the letter! Where was it? He jammed his hand into his pocket, no, not there! The other pants, he'd left them on the floor, but where were they now? He leapt from the bed and ran out the door just as his mother came through the living room toward him.

"Lucky for you I just started a load of wash," she said. "You'd a looked a sorry sight going to Sunday-school like that." She gave him a look that stopped short of forgiveness but lacked anger. "Here's your pocket knife from your pants, and there's a tuna-fish sandwich on the table for you."

"Mom, I had a piece of paper folded up in one of my pockets. Did you find it?"

"No I didn't, and if it was in your pocket, it's gone now." She said.

Alan ran out to the back porch and, pushing the wringer aside, lifted the lid of the sloshing Bendix and fished out his sopping-wet pants; there was nothing in any of the pockets. Back in his room he got down on the floor and looked under everything that might conceal the letter but it just wasn't there. Had he pulled anything from his pocket on the way home, maybe losing the letter that way?

"Alan, get in here and eat this sandwich or I'm going to throw it out!" his mother yelled from the kitchen. "And what did Mrs. Mahalik want with you?"

He went into the kitchen and sat down at the table.

"She just gave me a letter from one of the kids in class who moved away," Alan said, deciding to tell the truth up to a point and get it over with. "But I lost it somewhere before I could even read it." The words caused more tears to well up in his eyes. "Then I saw Ralph Mooney and he called me a name and I got knocked down." Alan looked down at his hands, clasped in his lap.

"Well, I wouldn't worry too much about the letter. He'll probably write again when he doesn't hear from you," she said, "but you've got to stop this fighting! You hear me?"

"Yes ma'am."

Wolfing down the sandwich, he ran out to retrace his steps from the willows. He followed his path as closely as he could remember it, his eyes fixed on the ground, picturing Michelene in his mind as well as he could. Was she thinking about him the way he thought about her? He could visualize her dark eyes and her face and hair. He thought about how thin she was and tried to remember the dresses she wore. A little ache settled on his heart as he thought about the letter and how he hadn't read even one word of it.

Searching, searching by every rock, in every patch of weeds, even picking up scraps of paper that obviously weren't it; he made his way back to the willow thicket, entering cautiously in case Ralph and Billy had returned. No one there; he scoured the path going in and coming out—nothing. He walked back up the hill past Shorty Nick's, a couple of cars there but not Curly's, nothing along the way that could be his letter.

Alan returned home dejected, wondering what to do. Should he get Michelene's address and write to her? Tell her he lost the letter and hope she would write back? He searched his bedroom again that night, stirring Ben's curiosity. Finally, he decided to enlist Ben in his search.

"It's a secret, Ben. If you find it and give back without telling anyone I'll give you a dollar!" Ben solemnly agreed

Alan tried to get back to normal. He and Two-Gun went to the town dump with their slingshots, targeting rats and bottles. They let Ben and his friend Charlie go with them to climb the mountain above the old mine shaft vents, clambering up slopes of loose, slippery coal shale to the base of the rocky cliffs. Ascending crab-like up crevices in the near-vertical cliffs, they clung to each hand-hold for dear life. They marveled at sea shells fossilized in the stone. From the top, the boys scanned the barren, desert vastness surrounding their little town and imagined they could almost make out the Pacific Ocean. On the way home they visited the old Basque shepherd tending his ragged flock of sheep and goats in the cedars north of town.

Every night though, Alan lay awake puzzling over what to do about the missing letter. He burned with curiosity about what Michelene might have said. Deep in the dark of the night he would imagine Michelene returning and asking why he had not replied to her letter. He would take her hand and tell her of the fight in the thicket and Curly's threats and his endless searches. She would weep for all he had suffered and put her arms around his neck, her tears moistening his face, and all would be well again.

Chapter 11

By the next Saturday, Alan could stand it no longer. He decided to write Michelene and tell her the letter had been lost and hope for a reply. He rode his bike to Mrs. Mahalik's house to get the address. Her room-mate answered the door.

"Oh, you're one of her students," she said. "Well, honey, she left for California a couple of days ago. Her husband was wounded and is in a hospital there." She smiled sympathetically at Alan's crestfallen expression. "She's going to stay with him a while. I don't know when she'll be back."

It seemed to Alan that everything was against him. He'd even tried praying, but so far it didn't look like God was going to help him either. His rational mind told him to give up on it. Who cares about some girl anyhow? Even if he found the letter it might just say how nice it was in Canada, so what? But, in fact, it had become an obsession with him. He had to find out about it, and her.

He steeled himself for the next logical step: going to the Dubois home to ask them for Michelene's address. What would they think? They didn't know him and might suspect he was up to no good. Well, it had to be done.

He rode his bike across the little park past the neglected tennis court to Grassy Trail Drive. He considered several approaches: Hello, I'm Alan Steger from Michelene's class and I've been asked by her friends to get her address so we can write to her. Hello, I'm here for Mrs. Mahalik to get Michelene's address for a class letter to her. Hello, I'm Alan … He was in front of the house.

Alan parked his bike and walked hesitantly up to the door. He knocked lightly and waited, rehearsing his question under his breath. Maybe they didn't hear him. He knocked harder, waited a minute and knocked again. Was that an echo of his knock? There it was again, only it sounded like someone tapping on glass. He stood there, puzzled, and raised his fist to knock again.

"Boy! You there!" The voice was crackly and high-pitched. Alan looked up at the second floor.

"Hoo there, boy, over here!"

Alan turned and saw the open window of the house next door. A very old man was motioning at him from inside. An Indian blanket covered the old man's shoulders, though the weather was quite warm. Dark shadows obscured his eyes and hollowed out the cheeks of his face. Alan walked hesitantly toward the window.

"What'cha want, boy?" the old man asked, extending a trembling hand over the window sill.

"I'm looking for the Dubois's," Alan replied, shrinking back a bit. "I, uh, have a message for them."

"Well, give it ta me. They've gone fer th' summer." The old man demanded in his crackly voice, "I'll give it ta 'em when they get back."

"Could you just tell me when they're coming home?" Alan asked, no longer surprised by disappointment.

"Yer a purty thang, ain't ya?" A wide toothless grin spread across the ancient countenance. "Ya lookin' fer that little gal 'at use ta live there?" This followed by a fit of hacking coughs. "Come closer so I can get a little look at ya," he continued, again reaching a long, bony hand over the sill toward Alan. "Jes' take my hand a minute."

"I gotta go!" Alan said, surprised and disgusted.

"They're French, ya know," the old man continued in his rasping, wheedling voice. "They mighta gone back to France. Might be gone a long time, jes' tell me what it is an' I'll tell 'em."

Faint specs of light deep in the sockets were the only evidence that eyes still peered from the dark, sunken features. Alan felt his skin crawl. "I'll just come back later," he said, backing away toward his bike.

"Ya better watch out, boy!" The old man's face collapsed into a deep frown. He pulled the window shut with an audible grunt.

Chapter 12

Wayne had been on the job more than a month. So far, he'd spent little time with the sheriff except for short meetings to talk about specific issues. Finally, he'd been invited to meet Tex for breakfast, a chance to get better acquainted with the man. Wayne arrived early and walked across the street from the courthouse to Crandall's Diner.

Tex met him at the door and shook his hand. "How're you doing this morning, Wayne?"

"Good and you?"

They walked inside. The smell of coffee, fried eggs and bacon filled the air, mixing with tobacco and cooking smoke that formed a greasy haze. They found their way to the sheriff's regular booth and took their seats.

The sheriff gave Wayne a friendly smile. "How's it going so far? You getting acquainted around with the folks you need to know?"

"I am," Wayne replied. "The people at the office are fine, except for a couple of holdouts. I don't think they'll be a problem. And, I've been down to the army's supply depot in Green River to meet with the provost marshal, Major Hudson. He called asking someone from here to come down."

"I know, been trying to avoid him. They got a big problem with thefts of everything from car tires to butter that's making its way to the black market. Most of it's going to Provo and Salt Lake, though some does end up here. Anyway, it's the kind of thing that takes a lot of work. We don't have enough people to do much."

"I figured that. Told him we'd try to help but didn't make any promises."

The waitress arrived and took their orders. Wayne looked around the place. "For a coal mining town," he said, "I haven't seen many coal miners, least not far as I know."

"You won't see them down town much. When you do, you'll be able to tell." Tex took a sip of coffee and leaned back as his breakfast was put in front of him. "We'll be going out to meet the folks who run General Coal here the end of this week. It's not the only coal company in town, but the biggest and, as far as they're concerned, the only one that matters. It's owned by the railroad. Then, you need to get out and see some of the mines. Most are around here, but there's a couple out in the east county, Dragger and Sunnyside, owned by Kaiser Steel that are among the bigger operations."

The men turned their attention to the food in front of them and the conversation drifted to small talk about the weather and the people at the sheriff's office.

"Speaking of Dragger and the east county," Tex said, "we have a deputy, named Jim Wells who lives there. He comes in about once a week and let's us know what's been going on. I'd like you to try to get out there ever so often just to look in on things."

"Any particular problem?"

"Well, I expect Jim will tell you about the town constable in Dragger. Name's Curly Mayo. He's a drunkard and has no business being a lawman of any kind, but Dragger's a company town, also owned by Kaiser. He's a shirt-tail relative of some company big-shot and got hurt in a mine accident. They appointed him to work as a constable for the company before I came back. I'm afraid he's going to be trouble one of these days."

"We've had problems with special deputies and such in Phoenix. Sometimes, like now, with a war on, they're helpful if they're any good at all. But once in a while you'll get a ringer. Usually, it's drinking."

They finished the meal and the sheriff leaned forward as to get up. Wayne thought now might be the time to bring up a question that had buzzed around in his mind like a trapped bee for more than a week.

"I was wondering, Sheriff, if I could talk to you about a personal matter," he paused a moment, "well, at least semi-personal?"

"Sure, what's on your mind?"

"It has to do with Sadie, your secretary."

A frown crossed the sheriff's face for a moment replaced quickly by a slight smile. "What about her?"

"Well, I just wanted you to know what a fine job she's been doing helping me get settled in here."

"Glad to hear it."

"I just wondered," Wayne continued, getting suddenly warm around the neck, "if it would be a problem in your mind if I invited her out to dinner some evening, you know, to kinda say thank you?"

The sheriff smiled and said, "Something like that is your own business, Wayne, as long as it doesn't interfere with work."

"Thanks," Wayne said, "I'll see that it don't."

Returning to the office, Wayne found Sadie at her desk. He asked about some business at hand then went to the subject on his mind:

"Uh, Sadie," he began, his tongue getting suddenly thick.

"Yes, Wayne?" she looked at him, cool at first but softening as she noticed the difference in his voice.

"Well, Sadie, I just wanted to say thanks for all the help you've been helping me get started here." His words seemed to stumble over one another.

"You're very welcome, Wayne," a slight smile as she turned back to her work.

"What I was wondering was, well, would you let me buy you supper one evening?" His face turned very red. "I noticed they got a new pianist at the New Cardiff's restaurant."

She looked a little surprised. "Well, I don't know, Wayne. Are you sure?"

"Yes, yes I am. I just want to show you my appreciation if you'll let me."

"Wayne, that's not necessary. Would you mind if we don't a set time for it just yet?"

"No, uh, sure, whatever you say, Sadie. Just let me know when." He turned back to his work, disappointed and a little embarrassed.

Wayne hadn't heard from Inez. The letter remained unread, stuck away in a drawer somewhere in his apartment, he thought. He'd talked once with Bart on the phone without mentioning it.

Finally, his curiosity began to work on him. He'd meant to read the letter just to see what it was about; silly of him to have put it off like this anyway, he thought. But now, he couldn't find it. He searched the apartment, his jacket pockets and his car. He wondered if he'd lost it or thrown it out with the trash. It began to prey on his mind. How could a letter have just disappeared? Why had she written, about what?

After a month fretting about it, he called Bart. "Heard anything about Inez lately?"

"Nope," Bart replied. "You still wondering about her? That's one piece of business I'd forget about if I was you, Pard."

"You're right; just wondered because she sent me a letter a while back. I didn't bother to read it when I got it and now it's lost."

"Don't say." Bart was silent for a moment. "Well, just for your information, I heard she'd moved back to Nogales, to her folks."

"Guess that's good news."

"Yeah, forget her, Wayne. I know it's hard to do with women some times, but on this one, that's the only way to go."

Wayne hung up the phone and leaned back on the sofa. Damn, he thought, what the hell did I do with that letter? He'd really tried to put Inez out of his thoughts, consciously turning them elsewhere when she popped into his mind. An effort required all too often, he found. He had tried replacing any thoughts about Inez with some thought or hope for Sadie. She was just as pretty. Only problem, he had no real experience with her, yet; didn't really even know her. When it came to Inez, there was experience to spare and mostly unforgettable.

It wasn't the sex, Wayne thought, but then admitted it was. Inez in the darkness, black hair spread out on the pillow surrounding her luminous face like an ebony sunburst; her eyes, dark and passion filled. The image plagued him in his loneliness, usually followed by bitter regrets over the lies and manipulations she'd used to hold on to him and the destruction of his reputation. What had he done with that damned letter, and what had she said?

Chapter 13

It had been almost two weeks since Alan's encounter with Ralph and Billy in the willow thicket. He had seen Ralph once at the company store with his mother. They had exchanged looks but didn't speak. He heard that Billy was staying with an aunt in Price. Alan tried to put the incident behind him. He was afraid of Billy and wasn't sure what to do about him anyway. He thought he could handle Ralph and schemed on getting even with him. And he feared Ralph or Billy had in some way got hold of his letter, although he couldn't think how.

Another week passed and neither Mrs. Mahalik nor the Dubois's had returned. Finally, sitting alone in a swing at the little park one afternoon, it came to him that there was one other person in town who might know how to reach Michelene. Shirley McCann had been Michelene's closest, and maybe only, friend at school. It made sense that if Michelene wrote to him she would also write to Shirley. Alan didn't know where Shirley lived but he had seen her at the library a couple of times since school let out.

The town library sat next to the creek in a small wooden building below C section. Alan was one of the few regular patrons. Two-Gun had gone with him once but declined further visits complaining that it reminded him of school. Alan began stopping by the library at every opportunity, usually once or twice a day. Instead of checking out books, he sat at one of the small tables and read them there waiting for Shirley to come by. He planned to make his quest for information about Michelene seem as matter-of-fact as possible.

He went so far as to get books about France so he could make his inquiry seem coincidental. Hi Shirley, he imagined himself saying, I was just here reading about Paris, France. Oh, by the way, that French girl in our class last year, what was her name? Oh yeah, wonder what happened to her? And, he imagined, Shirley would reply, Oh, I just got a letter from her and she asked about you. I have her address right here if you'd like to write to her. To which Alan would nonchalantly say, Oh, well, let me have it and if I get time I'll think about it.

Shirley arrived at the library one morning just as Alan was walking out the door and he came to a sudden stop as she passed him. In his effort to speak to her without being obvious, he very obviously turned and followed her back in. While she was browsing the modest stacks he began a feigned search around one of the tables. In his effort to attract Shirley's attention by sliding the table and chairs around rather noisily, he instead caused Mrs. Hoppler, the librarian for the day, to become concerned.

"Alan, what is all the fuss about?" she asked, walking over to where he was down on his hands and knees searching intently.

"Oh, ah, I'm sorry ma'am." Alan tried to rise, bumping his head on the table. "I lost my pencil and thought it might be here," he said, disappointed that it was her and a little rattled by his own clumsiness.

"Well, be a little quieter." Just the three of them were there but a rule was a rule.

This did attract Shirley's attention but she reacted with a little smile and tossed her head in a way that had always annoyed Alan. But he noticed that her curly brown hair bounced and caught bits of sunlight from the windows and that she was wearing shorts and her bare legs were smooth and tan. His idea of striking up a conversation with her seemed more daunting somehow. Alan had recovered himself a bit as Shirley walked over to check out a book. He got up and followed her out the door.

"Hi Shirley," he said, trying to sound disinterested, "how's your vacation going?"

"Fine, thank you, and yours?" she replied, not looking at him.

"I'm fine too. I was just reading about Paris, France in there. Real interesting place, you ever read about it?" He spoke rapidly, his words devoid of inflection as he tried to follow his plan.

Shirley stopped and looked at him. "Well of course I have," she said, peering intently at him through her glasses.

"Well, say, didn't we have a French girl in our class?" he continued awkwardly.

"You know very well we did, Michelene Villiers. Everyone was so rude to her, including you, Alan!"

Shirley's rebuke surprised him. Did Michelene think he was rude, he wondered. "Well, I guess no one knows where she went, huh?"

"I do," Shirley said, giving her head another little toss. "She wrote me a letter."

"Oh yeah?" his voice jumped a bit. His plan was working, "what did she say?"

"Oh, not much, she just told me about living in Canada."

"Canada, huh, that all?" Alan could barely contain his anxiety.

"Yes," Shirley said, smiling curiously at him.

Now he was stuck. How could he get Shirley to give him Michelene's address without just asking for it outright? And if he did, why would he say he wanted it? Alan stood looking at Shirley, but not a word came to his lips.

"Well, bye now." Shirley walked to her bike, which was next to his, placed her book carefully in the basket and wheeled it around to leave.

"Wait!" Alan yelled. "I mean, uh, wait a minute," he said, trying to gain a little composure as he trailed after her to his bike. He rode alongside her, trying to think of some way to raise the question of Michelene's address without having to explain his reasons.

"Bet I can beat cha' to the top of the hill!"

"I don't want to race," Shirley said, looking at him, her eyes narrowed. "What do you want, Alan?"

Then, with a mischievous smile, she sped ahead of him as they approached the hill going up from the creek. She had passed the driveway to Nick's Saloon before Alan caught up with her and she stayed even with him until they reached the top and were on Grassy Trail Drive. There, she stopped her bike and caught her breath. Alan, just pulling ahead of her, wheeled around and came back beside her.

"That was pretty good for a girl," he allowed. "Course that being a Schwinn helped."

Shirley just smiled showing nice white teeth, which caused Alan to realize that even with glasses, she was pretty.

"That was fun!" she said, and looking up at the sun, added, "It's lunchtime; I have to go home now. Bye." She pedaled away leaving Alan standing there gazing after her trying to collect his thoughts. He did take note, however, that Shirley turned into the driveway of one of the big Grassy Trail Drive houses. Alan made his way home resolved to get Michelene's address from Shirley. He'd think of something.

Chapter 14

The Thursday night movie was a special event among the kids of Dragger during the summer months. It always paired a western and a mystery; a double feature for the price of a single movie.

"Oh boy, a cowboy and a m-murder!" Two-Gun said in happy anticipation as he, Alan and Ben headed over to get Ben's pal, Charlie, a small, chubby boy who always wore over-alls.

Each boy had thirty cents which would pay the ten cent admission with enough left for a soda and popcorn. This evening the movies were Lash Larue in *Stage to Laramie* and a *Bulldog Drummond* thriller. A crowd of kids had already gathered in front of the theater when they arrived. The theater manager, Art Romero, was a large young man who wore a built-up shoe that belied a withered right leg. He walked slightly sideways as he limped among the throng trying to maintain order.

With the usual pushing and fudging the boys found their places in line, savoring the smell of freshly popped popcorn wafting through the doorway. Alan was almost to the ticket window when he noticed Shirley standing just inside the lobby. She seemed to be with Janice Conway but she was talking to … Ralph! Worse, she was favoring Ralph with one of those smiles she had bestowed on him just yesterday. Alan, suddenly overcome by a fit of jealousy, broke from the line, strode through the door past the manager, who was now taking tickets, and stopped between Shirley and Ralph. He stood there, glaring first at her and then at him, speechless with anger.

"Hey, pretty boy!" Ralph exclaimed with a surprised look, then frowning, "What do you want?"

"Take that back!" Alan yelled, throwing a roundhouse right at Ralph that landed on his chest driving him back against the candy counter.

"Now you're gonna get it!" Ralph snapped, regaining his balance and raising his fists.

They were immediately surrounded by the other kids filling the lobby. The manager clawed his way through and grabbed Alan by his shirt collar, dragging him backwards out the door.

"That's it kid! You're outta here and don't come back for two weeks!" Art shoved Alan toward the street and turned back to the throng in the lobby. "Break it up and get to your seats or there won't be a show tonight!"

Ben, Two-Gun and Charlie crowded around Alan.

"Wh-whatcha gonna do, Alan?" asked Two-Gun. "You w-want us to sn-sn-sneak you in the side door?"

"No, you guys just go on. I don't feel like watchin' no show now anyhow." Alan's head slumped and he jammed his hands in his pockets, deeply mortified over the way he must have looked in front of Shirley.

He walked a few steps away, stopping at the edge of the side walk. He looked up the street past the post office and barber shop to the company store where the town's only pavement came to an end. The street light above the intersection had just been turned on. Farther west, the sun was slipping behind the rugged silhouette of the Wasatch Mountains. He wondered what lay beyond that sunset and how he might get there. Across the highway a long train of coal cars slowly and noisily began its journey to distant furnaces. He thought how easy it would be to trot over and jump on one of those cars and ride it to some far off place where nobody knew him. Everything he tried had failed. All he wanted was to find Michelene's letter and all he'd found was disappointment.

"Alan?" Shirley's voice behind him.

He turned sharply, surprised and embarrassed. "Oh, hi, what do you want?"

"Well, Alan, I was wondering the same thing about you," she said earnestly. "Why did you do that back there?"

Alan looked at Shirley and noticed Janice standing behind her. He didn't know the answer to her question and he didn't want to talk to her in front of the other kids still in line for their tickets.

"I gotta go now, Shirley." He turned and walked up the street to the store where a clerk was locking up for the night. He stopped and looked back at the theater. Shirley and Janice had apparently gone inside, as had Two-Gun, Ben and Charlie.

Art Romero stood at the curb leaning down at the window of a car. He straightened up and pointed toward Alan. The car pulled slowly away from the theater moving toward him. It came to a stop at the curb.

"Come over here, boy," Curly Mayo called out to him.

Alan hesitated a moment then walked over and leaned down at the passenger side window.

"Open the door and get in," said Curly, sober this evening.

"Yessir." Alan got in, wincing at the sour, stale odors of tobacco and indigestion. He sat with his head down, hands folded in his lap.

"Art tells me you started a fight back there at the picture show," Curly said, re-lighting the dead stogie he'd been chewing on. "That right?"

"Yessir," Alan replied softly. "I'm sorry."

"Said the boy you punched was Ralph Mooney. That right?"

"Yessir."

"Well, you sure pick good enemies." Curly stuck his lighter back in his shirt pocket. You know you could get in a lot of trouble startin' fights, don't ya?"

"Yessir, I won't do it again."

"I'm glad to hear that. Course, that don't make it all right." Curly gave Alan a sidelong glance while taking a long draw on the stinking cigar. "You ain't gonna be able to go back to the picture show for a couple a weeks, so that's kinda like payin' your debt, I guess. But I'm gonna have to keep an eye on you for a while. You understand?"

"Yessir."

Curly exhaled another plume of smoke, filling the car with a pungent haze. "You want a ride home?"

"No! Uh, I mean, no thank you, sir." An image flashed into Alan's mind of his mother seeing him being brought home in the constable's car.

"Okay, one more thing," Curly said. "Your pal Ralph, back there, has a buddy named Billy Preston. You know him?"

Alan tensed. "No sir. I, uh, I've heard his name."

"Well, if you run across him, I want you to come tell me. You hear?" Curly fixed his gaze on Alan for emphasis.

"Yessir." Alan opened the car door to get out.

"And don't you go startin' no fights with that ol' boy," Curly said, "or you'll find yourself in a real fix."

Alan watched the constable's old Ford pull away and rattle off in the general direction of Nick's Saloon. He wondered why Curly had asked about Billy. Surely it had nothing to do with the fight in the willows. He still hadn't told anyone about that.

Alan looked back toward the theater. The sidewalk was empty. He wandered around the small downtown area in the gathering darkness where, in addition to the store and theater, the clinic and fire station were located. Across a weed-choked vacant lot stood the chapel used on Sundays by the Protestants and Catholics at different hours. North of it, across a street and another lot, was the schoolhouse, first to tenth grades, the largest building in town. The Mormons used it for their services.

All of these buildings were connected by gravel-covered streets that led out to the housing areas. C Section, where Alan lived, lay on the north side of the little valley through which the nearly dry creek followed its course. The gloom of the evening stirred a pang of bitter remorse in Alan. It seemed Ralph had won again.

It was almost dark. Alan knew he had to go home and tell his mother what had happened at the theater. He tried to still his qualms and began rehearsing his explanation as he headed down the hill toward the creek.

Chapter 15

"Did ja get a wh-whippin'?" Two-Gun arrived earlier than usual the next morning to discover Alan's fate.

"Naw," Alan answered through the screen door, "just bawled out. But I've gotta chop enough kindlin' for a week before I can go anywhere today."

"Well, guess what?" Two-Gun drew closer. "Art made Ra-Ralph leave too!"

"Oh yeah?" Alan's eyes widened. "How come?"

"Cause of somethin' Curly Mayo told him," Two-Gun said, lowering his voice.

"What? What'd Curly say to cause Art to do that?"

"Well," Two-Gun looked to both sides of the narrow porch and leaned in close to the screen. "Benny Hicks says that M-Mike at the confe-confec—candy counter heard Art t-tell some grown-up that the sh-sheriff had Curly lookin' for B-Billy Preston who's a b-buddy of Ralph's, and so Art don't want no trouble, ya know, s-so he kicks Ralph out r-right in the middle of Lash LaRue!" Two-Gun paused for effect but Alan's reaction was strangely quiet.

So that was what Curly was asking him about last night. Why, he wondered, was the sheriff looking for Billy? It must be serious. Curly usually took care of the regular mischief around town to the extent that anyone did.

"I'll see you after lunch, Two-Gun. I've gotta get that kindlin' cut."

Alan went to the wood stack next to the coal bin in back of the house and laid into his task. As he worked, chopping at the old two-by-fours and cedar logs with a rusty hatchet, he went over the events of the past few weeks from the time he got Michelene's letter and encountered Billy and Ralph in the willows. Whatever the sheriff wanted with Billy could have nothing to do with him. But as he thought about it, the desire for revenge that had been eating at him all this time took on a new fervor: revenge against Billy for putting him in fear of his life, and revenge against Ralph for his part in it and for causing him to humiliate himself in front of Shirley.

He finished cutting and stacking the kindling and, with grudging agreement from his mother that he'd met the terms of his punishment, headed for the park looking for Two-Gun.

The park was less than the word implied: a triangular lot about two acres in size with dilapidated swings, see-saws, a slide and a green-painted wood telephone booth, all clustered at one end next to a neglected tennis court. The rest, containing remnants of last year's victory gardens, had been abandoned to weeds and debris.

Alan found Two-Gun slumped listlessly in one of the swings and took the swing next to him. He began gliding slowly back and forth.

"You think there's a reward out for Billy?" he asked off-handedly.

"D-D-Don't know," Two-Gun replied, suddenly alert. "There m-might be though, huh?"

"You know what? If there was we could get it if we found out where Billy was hidin' and showed Curly."

"R-Really, how do ya know?"

"Cause, it's the law, that's how," said Alan with a conviction supported only by his imagination.

"How'll we f-find out if there's a r-reward?"

"I'll do it," Alan said, his mind racing through possible ways. "Listen, Two-Gun, you start seein' what you can find out about where Billy might be, but don't let on to nobody what we're doin', see, and I'll find out how much the reward is. Okay?"

"We're gonna be like d-detectives, huh?"

"Yeah, just like Bulldog Drummond."

It didn't take long for Alan to think of the post office as a source of information. He imagined a poster with Billy's photo hanging on the bulletin board. His recent disappointment had hardened him, so when he discovered the federal government was still unaware of Billy Preston's crimes, he merely shrugged and headed for the library. Copies of the Salt Lake Tribune, the Deseret News and the Collier Sun-Advocate were kept there for weeks.

Riding up to the library, Alan saw Shirley's bike parked in front. He felt a momentary urge to keep going. He was still embarrassed about the scene at the theater.

Shirley was sitting at a table reading when he walked in. She looked up and smiled. Alan blushed, shyness stilling his tongue. He looked at her, a little bewildered, and made his way around to the shelves where newspapers were kept. He sat down and began pulling out copies.

"Are you all right, Alan?" Shirley asked in the softest voice he'd ever heard from her. She had left her table and walked around to where he was sitting.

"Yeah," he replied, looking up. "I'm okay. Are you mad at me for last night?"

She stepped closer and leaned over, placing her hand gently on his shoulder, and in her still tender voice said, "I'm not mad at you Alan." Then she straightened up, turned and walked out the door.

Alan felt a warm, tingling sensation that began where she'd touched him and radiated throughout his body; his mind reeled.

Chapter 16

The next morning Alan and Two-Gun met in the park.

"G-G-Guess what," Two-Gun said as they pulled their bikes alongside one another. "I think I f-found where Billy's h-hidin' out!"

"Oh yeah," Alan replied, surprised at such quick results, "where?"

"In the willows, d-down below Nick's Saloon; you know, where all the kids u-used to hide out 'til everybody got tired of it."

Mention of the willows caused a tremor of anxiety in Alan's mind, but he shook it off.

"The willows don't sound like a good hideout to me. Are you sure?" He gave Two-Gun a doubtful look.

"I s-seen R-Ralph come outta there y-yesterday afternoon when I was going to the school," Two-Gun replied, a little miffed at the response. "I watched him p-practically run to the store and get a b-bag of gr-gr-stuff and take it back to the willows," he said speaking louder to make his point. "S-So he had to be takin' food or something to Billy, don'tcha see?"

Alan looked at Two-Gun a moment, a little peeved himself, and said, "Well, didja see Billy go in or come out? How about Ralph? How long was he in there?"

"L-Look, I had to g-get home to supper, b-but I betcha Ralph was takin' supplies to Billy. What else w-would he be doin' in there?"

"Okay," Alan said, realizing there was no point in arguing. "That could be right. Maybe we oughtta set up a lookout there."

"Wh-what about the r-reward?"

"Oh, yeah, well I ain't sure how much it's gonna be yet," Alan said, furrowing his brow. "But I did find out what I think the sheriff wants Billy for. It was in the Collier paper. Last week a guy was held up by someone with a knife." Alan paused, "Everybody knows that's something Billy would do, so that's it, probably."

"That d-don't sound like no b-big reward case to me," Two-Gun said testily. "I ain't g-gonna sit around on no l-lookout if there ain't no reward in it."

"Ain't 'cause you're chicken, huh?" Alan, offering a sneer, put the kickstand down on his bike and got off.

"D-don't you call me no ch-chicken 'less you're ready to back it up, you ..."

"You what?"

"You know." Two-Gun stepped off his bike and leaned it against the swing.

"Know what?"

"M-maybe you'd like to f-find out." Two-Gun gave Alan a shove.

"You want a punch? You're gonna get one." Alan responded, his temper rising.

"Wait!" Two-Gun yelled, "Code of the West!" Invoking the code bound both parties to settle their quarrel according to pre-set rules. "I g-get first punch."

"You started it, which means I get first punch." Alan took a pugilist stance.

Two-Gun stood his ground. "The r-rule is the one who st-starts a fu-fuss has to let the o-other one take first punch. Y-you called me a ch-chicken. That started it, so st-stand still."

Alan considered the argument for a moment and reluctantly straightened up. "Shoulder or stomach?"

"Stomach," Two-Gun said grimly. Then, reconsidering, said, "No, sh-shoulder."

Two-Gun's punch, thrown with all his strength, landed squarely on Alan's shoulder with a bruising sting, knocking him atilt and sending him hopping a couple of steps.

"Okay, y-your turn," Two-Gun pulled the sleeve of his T-shirt up baring his shoulder.

Alan took his swing, a wide right that struck a glancing blow off Two-Gun's shoulder, barely moving him.

"Sissy punch," Two-Gun gloated.

"You flinched! You're the sissy!"

"Did not! Ain't my f-fault you can't hit straight." Two-Gun stood back with a contemptuous smirk.

Alan lunged forward tackling him, both landing on the gravel and weed-covered ground grunting and grappling for advantage. The wrestling lasted less than a minute before Two-Gun's nose began bleeding, smearing them both. At the sight of blood Alan jumped back.

"You're bleeding all over the place, Two-Gun!"

"Don't hurt none; I-I ain't givin' up!"

"Well, I'm callin' King's X, on account of blood," Alan said, standing up and wiping his hands against his pants.

"Okay," Two-Gun got to his feet using his T-shirt to staunch his nosebleed.

The boys stood silent for a moment, allowing their tempers to subside.

"You wanna go to the schoolyard and see if we can get in a ball game?" Alan asked.

"Okay," Two-Gun replied, "b-but what about our c-case?" a note of disappointment in his voice.

Alan was disappointed too. "I'll see what else I can find out then we'll do something,"

After the dizzying encounter with Shirley in the library, Alan had finally managed to regain his senses enough to finish going through the papers for the previous three weeks. The robbery at knifepoint was the only crime other than a few drunken assaults and black market investigations he could find. He felt his plan to bring Billy to justice might be unraveling. Besides, the idea of playing the informant ruffled his conscience a bit. He needed to think more about this.

They headed toward the school, sauntering along, hands in pockets except when Alan stopped to sail a rock over a house or at a utility pole. They looked at nothing in particular and broke the silence with whistled bird-calls and some nameless sounds.

Alan took note as they passed Shirley's home but saw no one about. A little further along, they came to the Dubois house; there was still no sign they had returned. Next door, in the driveway, backed in between the houses so that it wasn't immediately visible, sat a black Cadillac hearse. Alan and Two-Gun both gasped when they saw it. They knew what it meant, and the fact that it was seldom seen in town lent a certain macabre excitement to the discovery. The constable's car was parked across the street.

"Jesus and Mary," said Two-Gun, crossing himself.

"Bet I know who died," Alan said quietly.

"Who?"

"There's a real old man lives there, used to."

"Oh y-yeah, y-you know who else lives there? R-Ralph, that's who!"

That piece of information came as a shock to Alan. He knew Ralph lived in C Section but had refused to care enough about him to find out where. The realization wormed its way into his conciousness that Ralph had lived next door to Michelene all that time, and he'd never thought of them even knowing one another outside of class. He wondered if they had spent time together. All of it: Ralph and Shirley and now Ralph and Michelene; the possibilities crowding into his mind set off spasms of jealousy and despair. This on top of the evidence of death in their midst caused Alan to feel a sudden surge of nausea. He wanted to go home, find a refuge from all these feelings.

As the boys stood there, a sheriff's car pulled up behind Curly's and a khaki-clad deputy got out and crossed the street to the old man's house.

Chapter 17

Wayne Carleton parked his dusty, green '38 Buick in the lot next to the courthouse.

He was running late. The meeting with the provost marshal down at the Army Supply Depot had lasted longer than expected. Today was Wayne's forty-fifth birthday, same age as the century he liked to say, and the sheriff had promised to buy his lunch. Sadie met him at the door.

"Sheriff wants you to meet him over at Beisner's," she said. "Doc Clary called a little while ago; thinks he's got a murder." She gave him a big smile, "By the way, happy birthday!"

"Thanks, want to help me celebrate with dinner at the New Cardiff tonight?"

A bright smile lit up her face. "What a good idea, let's talk about it when you get back."

Wayne spotted the sheriff limping back and forth in front of Beisner's Funeral Parlor. He was aware of Tex's squeamishness when it came to dead bodies of any kind. If this was a murder, an autopsy would be required and he knew Tex wouldn't get through that.

"Morning Sheriff," Wayne said, extending his hand.

"It's about time," Tex replied, smiling.

"This don't look like lunch to me," Wayne said, deadpan.

"Well, no, I reckon not." Tex grinned. "Doc Clary called me this morning. They had a death out in Dragger yesterday, an old man. Jim Wells thought it was from natural causes, but Doc found something in his throat that choked him and he thinks it might have been forced there."

They were met in the funeral parlor lobby by an obsequious attendant in a faded, black suit who directed them down a hallway past the musty, floral smells of the visitation room.

They found their way back to a curtained alcove set up as a surgery for the coroner. Entering the small room, barely larger than the autopsy table, the cloying odor of formaldehyde and tobacco fumes from Doc's pipe caused both men to wince and catch their breaths.

Doc Clary greeted them heartily, wiping his hand on his old rubber apron before reaching out over the corpse to shake theirs. A stout man in his sixties with thick, unruly gray hair that seemed to stand straight up on his head, Doc was a practicing physician as well as the county's coroner.

The emaciated body lay on the autopsy table; all but the head covered with a sheet. A wood carving board, on which was spread an array of knives that looked like they could have come from any well equipped kitchen, rested on the sheet over the cadaver's pelvic area. After a few pleasantries, Doc got down to business.

"First," Doc said, "you know Curly Mayo called me yesterday evening to say he thought there might be something funny about this case, and that's in spite of your deputy, Jim Wells, writin' it up as a natural causes."

"Now that is something," Wayne said, "Curly's not known for bein' a great observer."

A disgusted look crossed Tex's face. "You might make sure Jim Wells hears about this, Wayne, when you see him."

"I will, after I talk with Curly."

"Anyway," Doc said, turning their attention back to the corpse, "you can tell by the way the epiglottis is distended and from the scraped tissue, that this paper was forced into his throat." Doc held up a small, wadded ball of paper which he placed on a side table.

"Look here, you can see for yourselves." He pointed the beam from a small flashlight into the cadaver's toothless mouth, wagging its now dislocated jaw.

Wayne peered in while Tex fixed his eyes on a wall calendar depicting the Mormon Tabernacle in Salt Lake City.

"Really, all you'd a had to do to kill him would a been to hold your hand or something over his mouth and nose a few seconds." Doc interrupted himself for a series of deep, mucous laden coughs, then, wiping his mouth with a handkerchief, wheezed on. "He had the black lung so bad he was hardly breathing anyway. Also, there's a little string burn on his neck. Don't know if that's anything."

The fatal piece of paper was flattened out to reveal a message written in ink in a small, neat hand. There were remarkably few stains considering its former location and other than creases and wrinkles, it was undamaged.

"A letter of some sort, looks like," said Doc, adjusting his spectacles.

Wayne and Tex both examined the paper. Wayne held it up to the light look-ing it over closely.

"If I was to make a guess, I'd say a kid wrote it." He frowned. "I don't see anything that'd make you want to shove it down anybody's throat."

He handed it back so the doctor could make a small identifying mark on it. Then Wayne placed it in a manila envelope which was initialed and dated by both of them to be saved as evidence.

"This whole thing seems mighty peculiar to me," Tex said as he and Wayne walked back to the courthouse. "Can you get on it right away?"

"Well, the provost marshal down at Green River is hot to get going on some motor oil thefts."

Tex looked at his pocket watch. "He's got a lot more folks working for him than I do. I expect he can spare you a little bit now and then."

"Whatever you say, boss. I'll work it out," Wayne replied.

Back at the sheriff's office, Wayne told Shirley he might have to post pone the birthday dinner. "Looks like a murder and I've got to go out to Dragger this afternoon. Can't say for sure how long I'll be." He waited for a response but she just looked at him. "Well, I mean, would you mind if we had the dinner Friday evening instead? We could take a little more time and enjoy it more."

"It's all right Wayne. Why don't we just wait until you can be sure?" she said, making it sound more like a statement than a question.

"That was pretty observant of you, Curly," Wayne said as the two of them talked over coffee in the little café next to the Dragger gas station. "What made you suspicious? Doc Clary said the old man was nearly dead anyway."

"Well," said Curly, eyes wide and protruding, pausing to reflect on and savor the rare praise. "It was the way he was sprawled out there next to his wheel chair. Just didn't seem to me the way he'd end up if he died natural. It was more like he was tossed there."

Wayne leaned back and looked at his cup. "Seems funny to me Jim Wells didn't see that; did you mention it to him?"

"I did, but he wasn't payin' me much attention. Seemed like he was in a hurry and just wanted to get finished."

Wayne was aware of the low esteem in which Curly was held by Deputy Wells. He'd filed a report within the past month complaining about finding Curly drunk on duty. It wasn't surprising that he might ignore the constable's opinions.

"I expect that was it, he was probably in too much of a rush," Wayne said, leaning forward. "But you were right, Curly. Do you have any notions about who might have done it?"

"I do! You know that kid Billy Preston you all were lookin' for a couple of weeks ago?" Curly fixed his bulging eyes on Wayne. "Well, he's been runnin' with the old man's grandson, Ralph Mooney, for some time now. I just think it figures that a kid like that'd have something to do with it."

"Maybe, but all we had on him was bein' a runaway from his aunt; although she did tell us that he had a record back in Kentucky. If he is involved we've gotta have evidence of some kind to tie him to it." Wayne tipped his Stetson back, glancing around to see if anyone was in earshot.

"Curly, I'm investigating this as a murder now and I could use your help, but you've gotta be careful that whatever you do is by the book. A mistake with the evidence could really mess us up. And, by the way," Wayne motioned Curly in closer and lowered his voice. "Don't say anything about this bein' a murder for now. Do you understand?"

Curly nodded vigorously. The Undersheriff's new attitude toward him seemed to give Curly a sense of importance that had not existed before. "Don't worry Wayne, I'll be careful and keep in touch with you about anything I find out."

Wayne had planned to see Deputy Wells and go by the Mooney home, but it was getting late and he had work to do at his office. Sadie, much to his disappointment, had left before he got there. He returned to his small apartment well after dark. Each time, almost without thinking, he gave the place a quick once-over for the missing letter before settling in to his evening routine.

He could say to the hour, almost to the minute, how long Ruth had been gone. His social life which, not counting Inez, never amounted to much, had shrunk to almost nothing since his move to Collier. An old saying: "once burned, twice learned," kept him shy about women and was the reason it had taken him so long to approach Sadie.

It had become his habit to sit down every night before going to bed and write a letter to Paul, still somewhere in the Pacific. At the end of the week, he'd choose one that seemed newsy and cheerful and mail it. The others, which he realized were really to Ruth, he burned in the fireplace, a smoky offering to her memory.

The phone rang.
"Hey Pard, how's it going?" Bart Ramirez's voice.
"Hi, Bart, I'm just getting ready for bed."

"Bed, all alone? You have settled down. It's only nine O'clock." A moment of silence, "Guess you haven't stirred up a girl friend yet."

"That would be a pretty good guess. I've been keeping busy with work," Wayne said, Sadie's face flashing in his mind's eye.

"Far be it from me to tell you how to live your life, but don't you think it's about time to find some nice, respectable woman to show you how to spend your spare time?"

"Probably, but they ain't to be found just anywhere, you know," Wayne said, a little annoyed.

"Okay," Bart said. "I've been trying to decide whether or not to tell you this, but guess I should."

"Tell me what?"

"We, me and Dolores, ran into Inez the other night down in Tucson."

"Oh, she have anything to say I should know about?" An empty spot opened in Wayne's stomach.

"No, as a matter of fact, she didn't mention you." Bart paused and Wayne could sense he was taking a drag on a cigarette. "Just said she was working at a lodge up on Mount Lemon and that everything was fine."

"Doing what? At the lodge, I mean."

"Singing; said she'd hooked up with a piano player and they had been working the clubs. What she was doing when you met her, I think."

"Yeah, that all?"

"We didn't talk long. Dolores, you know."

"Well, that sounds like a good sign to me," Wayne said.

The conversation lasted a few more minutes. Afterwards, Wayne wondered again about the letter Inez had written to him. Was it stuck in some out of the way corner around the apartment, or in his desk at work? So thoroughly had he searched all those places, he doubted it was still around.

Chapter 18

Alan and Two-Gun had all but given up their plan to find Billy and turn him in. The death in Ralph's family, still thought to be from natural causes, and the absence of a reward, had dampened their enthusiasm. Alan had also been distracted by Shirley's interest in him and his new-found attraction to her. He had never felt this way about a girl. Unlike his almost entirely imaginary relationship with Michelene, Shirley was right there with him, responding to him and him to her.

They had begun meeting at the library where they would share a table and books of mutual interest.

"What are you going to do when you're grown, Alan?" Shirley asked him one morning.

"I'm gonna be a pilot in the Army Air Corps," Alan responded without hesitation. "Just like my Uncle Jack."

"Ooh," said Shirley, wide-eyed. "That sounds so dangerous. But by then the war'll be over so at least no one will be shooting at you."

"Even if they do, it won't stop me!" Alan sat a little straighter and set his jaw. "I ain't scared of nothing like that."

"Anything like that," Shirley corrected.

"That's right," Alan said a little smugly. "And if there's a war then I'll win me some medals, just like my Uncle Jack's got."

"Well, if you get hurt I'll take care of you because I'm going to be a doctor."

"You mean a nurse. Girls are nurses."

"Not me," Shirley replied primly. "I'm going to be a doctor."

"Aw, I never heard of a woman doctor. I don't think there is any such thing."

"There is too!" Shirley said with some heat. "Doctor and Mrs. Voss have dinner at our house ever so often, and when I told him I wanted to be a doctor he said that was just fine because there were some very good women doctors around now and with the war there'll be a lot more."

"Well, I never heard about any women doctors before."

Shirley folded her arms on the table and looked at him as if he were a cute but troublesome puppy.

He noticed the soft roundness of her face and form, her smooth, unblemished skin and her lively way of talking, all contrasting sharply with his lean angularity, all sinew and bone marked with scrapes and bruises, and his tendency to lapse into awkward silences.

They prowled the narrow aisles of the library stacks, looking for books to share. She reached for one on an upper shelf but couldn't quite grasp it.

"Let me." Alan reached up, brushing against her, and brought it down. She took it slowly, looking in his eyes with a softness and openness he had never seen. His knees went weak, wobbling, as if an electric current had passed through. He stumbled and leaned against her. Neither of them moved. They stood, touching for a long, silent moment.

These times with Shirley eroded Alan's usual reserve enough for him to want to hold her hand, though briefly and not when anyone was watching. But they had been seen together. Two-Gun, especially, had begun to question what was happening to his best friend.

"Benny Hicks said Terry Boyle s-seen you and Sh-Shirley sittin' together at the show Tuesday night," he said one day as they explored the nearly dry creek bed looking for bottles and other valuables.

"We, uh, I mean I guess I did see her there," Alan replied trying to hide a pang of guilt. "So what?"

So, is sh-she gonna be your g-girl friend?" Two-Gun's question contained hints both of hurt and jealously. The boys were becoming aware of a change stealing silently upon them. They had seen its effect on older friends but refused to admit that they too would succumb. Both had vowed not to have anything to do with girls until they were grown and married.

"Don't worry, Two-Gun, we're blood brothers and always will be, remember?" They had declared themselves so after acting out an Indian ritual they'd seen in a movie. Two-Gun shrugged and let the matter drop.

Alan's feelings of guilt went beyond his concerns for Two-Gun. His thoughts about Michelene were becoming vague and less frequent. When he tried to visualize her face, Shirley's would appear. He had abandoned the notion of asking Shirley for Michelene's address and now contended with stirrings of conscience over a sense of disloyalty. A latent anxiety smoldered in him along with a perception that something precious was slipping away. Unable to focus on the root of his dilemma, he put it aside to consider another day.

The boys made their way down the rocky, nearly dry creek bed, stopping to inspect the dank, stagnant pools in boulder-shaded bends and dark grottos beneath old cottonwoods and thick juniper. At various intervals, narrow paths, little more than game trails, snaked up the steep hillside through dense sage brush to the back yards of the big houses on Grassy Trail Drive. They passed the library, on the other side of the creek, and then were at the roadway and across it into the willow thicket. Alan cringed a little every time he came near this place, still marked by his experience here with Ralph and Billy.

They went in, passing the spot where the fight had occurred, and on into the cave-like hollow. It was littered with trash: odd bits of clothing, a Montgomery Wards catalogue and other pieces of scrap paper and food wrappers.

"L-looks like some hobo's been l-living here," said Two-Gun. "Betcha it was Billy."

"Me too," Alan responded, again thinking of turning him in.

They passed through the willows to the bottom of the slope that lead up to the back of Nick's Saloon parking lot. They scoured the area for beer bottles tossed down by patrons of the saloon. Normally, they would then climb to the parking lot and grab any bottles in sight but Alan demurred.

"Wh-what's the matter?" asked Two-Gun.

"I don't think we oughtta go there anymore," Alan said, remembering Curly's drunken admonition.

"Why not? That's where m-most of the bottles are!" Two-Gun said, suspicion shading his voice. But he followed glumly as Alan began making his way back toward the road. Coming out of the willows they saw a large green Buick drive by, little swirls of dust trailing its wheels as it climbed the hill to Grassy Trail Drive.

Chapter 19

"I just can't believe it," Mrs. Mooney said, dabbing her eyes with a hanky. "It just can't be murder! Who'd do it? He never hurt anyone. He didn't hardly know a soul out here."

Wayne couldn't help but notice that Mrs. Mooney was a nice looking woman. His mental warning came on immediately and he studiously avoided further thoughts in that direction.

"I'm real sorry, ma'am," Wayne said taking a seat at the kitchen table and putting his hat and briefcase on a chair. "I'm going to have to ask you a few questions." He reached in the battered old briefcase and took out a green stenographer's notebook. Pulling his chair up to the table, he jotted down the time and date. "Now, according to Deputy Wells' report, your son, Ralph, was the one who found your father's, uh, found him. Is that right?"

"Well, yes. I had gone to Collier and when I got home Ralph was out in the front yard, very upset, and he told me Papa was dead."

"And is Ralph at home now?"

"Upstairs, but, Sheriff, he's been through a lot over Papa's passing and I think if you're going to tell him about it being a murder," she shuddered at the word, "then I think his father should be here. Mr. Mooney will be home pretty soon."

"While we're waiting, let me ask you another question," Wayne spoke almost indifferently. "Do you know a boy named Billy Preston?"

"Billy is my nephew. My sister, his mother, died back home in Kentucky and he was sent out here to stay a while. Why do you ask?"

"Sorry to hear that ma'am; I'm just trying to get a picture of the circumstances. Did he ever live here in Dragger?"

An expression, fleeting as a shadow, crossed her face. "He stayed with us a while when he first came out but he's with my other sister in Collier right now." Her voice trailed off a bit. "At least he was staying there."

"And when was the last time you saw him here in Dragger?"

"About a week or so ago; of course then I didn't know he'd run away from Cora and he was by here just a few minutes with, uh, Ralph." Mrs. Mooney turned and looked away.

Mr. Mooney arrived as expected. After a brief, curtly received introduction, Wayne explained that Mr. O'Ryan's death was now considered a homicide.

"He choked to death on a piece of paper," Wayne explained, "and it appeared to have been forced down his throat."

Mr. Mooney looked doubtful. "Well, I have a real hard time with that," he said, scowling. "That don't make any sense at all."

"I know, it's a new one on us too," Wayne replied. "Now, I need to ask a few more questions since Deputy Wells wasn't aware of this when he was here."

Mrs. Mooney, unbidden, went to the foot of the stairs and called Ralph. He came down sullen faced and, after Wayne introduced himself, took a seat next to his father.

Wayne looked at Ralph. "Were you the only one here when you found your grandpa?"

"Yes sir," Ralph said meekly.

"And did you notice anything or anyone around that appeared unusual to you?"

"No sir."

Turning to Mr. and Mrs. Mooney, Wayne asked, "How about either of you? Anything unusual about the house, anything missing, any strangers been seen around just before or after the body was found?"

Both shook their heads but Ralph looked up, clearing his throat, "Uh, I seen two kids I know standing out on the street when your deputy came."

"And who were they?"

Ralph made another little grunting sound and said, "Alan Steger and Two-Gun, uh, that is, Henry Oakley."

"Mrs. Steger?" The large man standing on her front porch touched the brim of his hat. "I'm Wayne Carleton from the sheriff's office. I believe you have a boy named Alan?"

"Oh, my lord, what's happened?" she exclaimed, wringing her hands, "What's he done?"

"I'm not sure he's done anything, ma'am. We're just looking into some things involving a few of the boys here in town and his name came up. I'd just like to talk with him then I'll let you know if there's anything to worry about."

"Well, I expect he'll be home before too long. I mean, he knows to be home by supper time but he doesn't have to be here any sooner." She tugged at her apron. "He's probably out in the cedars somewhere."

"Thank you ma'am," Wayne said, lifting his Stetson and smoothing his hair. "I'll be going along for now. If I run into Alan I'll talk with him. Otherwise, I may have our deputy, Mr. Wells, stop by and set up a meeting for us."

Alan walked into the house at supper time, but feeding him was not his mother's first concern.

"Alan, you get in here this minute!" she yelled from the kitchen as he closed the door. "The sheriff was by here looking for you this afternoon and I want to know what you've got yourself into, right now!" Her voice rose with each word.

The sheriff? Alan couldn't imagine anything he'd done that would bring out the sheriff. The incident with Ralph and Billy came immediately to mind but he had told no one about that. The only other thing he could think of, the fight at the theater had been handled by Curly and didn't amount to enough to interest a sheriff anyway. He walked into the kitchen.

"I didn't do anything to get the sheriff after me," Alan said, as puzzled as his mother. "He must want to know about someone else."

"Well, I'm going to have to tell your dad about this and you'd better have a good answer for him. That sheriff's comin' back!" She turned to her stove. "And before I forget, you get out there and bring in some coal and kindlin'. It's just about all gone from the porch."

Grateful for the distraction, Alan set about gathering small bits of kindling and filling the coal bucket. Setting the bucket down on the porch he bumped the kindling box against the washing machine. Reaching to straighten it back, his eye fell on a small object lying in the space between the box and the wall. It was the little folded square of paper he had made of Michelene's letter. He almost cried out in his joy of discovery. The very thing that had sent him on his long and fruitless search of the last month had been here on the porch all the time. He felt like dancing a jig. His mom must have shaken it out of his pants pocket when she put them in the wash.

The little square of paper seemed even dirtier now than he remembered. He slowly and carefully unfolded it, a terrible sense of disappointment and sorrow overtaking him. This wasn't Michelene's letter. It just looked like someone's grocery list.

Chapter 20

Wayne began his day at the sheriff's office early. He liked to watch the sun coming up over the Tavaputs Plateau and the gradual lighting of the desert, its colors changing from a sooty burnt-umber to variegated shades of browns and grays speckled with dark green cedar, the creeks and arroyos marked by shiny cottonwoods. He'd just finished putting a pot of coffee on the hot plate in the outer office when the sheriff walked in.

"Well, morning Sheriff," Wayne said, a little surprised. "You're up early."

"Morning yourself," Tex replied, hanging his hat on the rack by the door. "You 'bout got that murder out in Dragger all wrapped up?"

"I would have if I'd known you were in a hurry for it. I might work a little faster if someone would buy my breakfast."

The two men walked in silence from the white brick courthouse, across its leafy square to Crandall's Diner.

The Sheriff paused at the diner's door, scratched at his chin and looked around as though searching for something. "The reason I asked about that case out in Dragger is that I got a phone call from the mine superintendent about it." Tex pushed the door open and they walked in.

The usual smells of coffee, cooking and tobacco smoke filled the air. A couple of miners sat in one of the booths and a man in rancher's attire sat alone at the counter. "Babe" Crandall, a stout, middle-aged man wearing an apron, nodded to them from the kitchen.

"George Hicks called me yesterday," Tex went on in his slow drawl. "He said one of his managers, Mr. Mooney, was upset about the way this case was being handled."

"That right?" Wayne frowned. "He say what the complaint was?"

"Just questioned the way we handled it, not finding out it was a murder in the first place and all."

"That can't be helped now. If you want, I'll stop by and talk to him."

"No, don't bother. I just mentioned it so you'd know." Tex limped over to their regular table with Wayne and they sat down. A waitress brought them coffee and took their orders.

Tex took a sip from his cup. "How about Curly, is he getting in the way?"

"No, I'm kinda surprised at him myself, but he's called me a couple of times, sober, and had done just what I asked." Wayne allowed a little grin. "Maybe we had the old boy all wrong."

"We had him right, all right, but maybe he's wised up a little," Tex said frowning. "Didn't you read Well's report about some of the miners at Nick's Place takin' Curly's gun and passing it all around the bar before giving it back?"

"I did," Wayne said disgustedly. "Just made me glad he works for the mine and not us."

Tex looked at Wayne shaking his head. "It ain't that simple. He still passes for what amounts to a peace officer and that reflects on us." The Sheriff finished his coffee. "I told the company superintendent out there I was gonna have the Board pull his commission if we had any more complaints about his drinking." He cast a glance back at the kitchen. "And I meant it!"

Their sausage and eggs arrived, and both ate in silence for a short while.

"Just so you know," Wayne said, "I'm going to Green River Army Depot this morning then back out to Dragger this afternoon. I've gotta try to run down a couple of kids and talk to them. One is that 'Alan' who that letter is to."

"He a suspect, you think?"

"Hard to say right now," Wayne finished his coffee. "The letter is the only real connection and that don't make sense yet."

"Well, give my regards to Major Hudson," said Tex with a wry smile. "By the way, when you're running down that black market stuff do you ever wonder how Crandall here manages to have all this good food for us."

"Nope," Wayne replied with a wide grin, patting his stomach, "and I ain't about to start."

Wayne parked in front of the Steger house about five o'clock, figuring it would be close to supper time and he might find Alan at home. Mrs. Steger answered the door, wiping her hands on her apron. Wayne could smell beans cooking in the kitchen.

"Evening, Mrs. Steger," he removed his hat and entered at her invitation. "I expect you know I'm here to see Alan if he's at home."

At that, Alan walked out of his bedroom looking expectantly at his mother.

"Alan, this is Sheriff Carleton and he wants to talk to you." She wrung her hands nervously. "You just tell him whatever he wants to know."

Wayne looked around the small living room, clean but sparsely furnished. The big, company issued coal stove sat against one wall. An old red sofa and easy chair with a coffee table between them made up the rest of the furnishings. Artie Shaw's arrangement of "Begin the Beguine" drifted from a table radio on a shelf next to the kitchen door. Wayne took a seat on the couch and set his briefcase and hat on the floor. He began with small talk about the weather and war news to settle things down. Then he got to the purpose of his visit.

"We've come to believe that Mr. O'Ryan, Mrs. Mooney's father," he looked at Alan, "Ralph's grandfather, did not die a natural death but was killed by someone." Wayne spoke in a quiet, matter-of-fact tone. "Did you ever meet Mr. O'Ryan, Son?"

Alan stared at Wayne, wide-eyed, mouth agape, speechless for what seemed like a long time. Then, "Yessir, well, he spoke to me once when I was at the house next door."

"And what were you doing there?"

At this, Alan hesitated, looked at his mother, his hands, then back at Wayne. "Well," he began, "I had lost a letter and I went there to get an address so I could write back."

"How would you get it at that house?" Wayne asked softly.

Alan hesitated again. He sat silently. No one spoke. The washing machine could be heard sloshing away on the back porch as they awaited his response. Finally, with his eyes beginning to tear, Alan told the story of his letter from Michelene; how he got it from Mrs. Mahalik, the fight with Ralph and Billy in the willows and his search for it afterwards. Wayne's gentle prodding brought forth enough details to provide a reasonably clear picture for him.

"What was in the letter you lost?" Wayne shifted in his seat and looked directly at Alan.

"Well," said Alan, a couple of tears beginning to glide down his cheeks, "I don't know. I never got a chance to read it."

Wayne leaned back, raising his eyebrows, "Would you recognize the letter if you saw it again?"

Alan's face drooped; he caught his breath, struggling, it seemed, to maintain his composure but failing and giving way to a burst of tears. He tried to speak but sobs interrupted. Then, regaining some control, he looked at Wayne. "I don't know," he said, his head dropping to his chest.

"Well, now, Sheriff, that's the truth," his mother interjected. "He told me the same thing a few weeks ago. I'll tell you this, Alan ain't perfect but he was raised to be honest."

"So you don't know what happened to the letter?" Wayne asked more or less rhetorically.

"I think Ralph or Billy got it," Alan replied and went on to explain about the paper he thought was the recovered letter.

"Do you still have that piece of paper?"

"Yessir, I'll get it." Alan ran into his bedroom and returned shortly with the smudged and crumpled page. He handed it to Wayne who carefully smoothed it out on the coffee table in front of him. It appeared to be mining company stationery. Imprinted at the top was: <u>Arthur R. Mooney, Transport Manager</u>.

Below the printing in rough penciled handwriting was a list for groceries: beans, crackers, peanut butter and one that caught Wayne's eye: candy—any kind.

I'd like to keep this if you don't mind," Wayne said, and without waiting for an answer, folded it and put it in his briefcase. "Alan, what you told me about the fight in the willows amounts to a felony assault. I want you to think real careful about what you said until you're sure it's the absolute truth. Then, if I take it down official, you may have to testify in court, under oath, about it. Now, anything you want to change?"

"No sir, that's what happened," Alan said without hesitation.

"Okay," Wayne got up and collected his hat and briefcase. "I'll be back to see you before long." He nodded to Mrs. Steger. "Try not to worry too much, ma'am, and it'd be better not to talk about this to anyone else right now." He gave Alan a serious look. "You either."

Chapter 21

Wayne sat in his car for a couple of minutes jotting down some notes in the steno pad before pulling away from the Steger home. It was after six but still daylight. He wondered what Curly might be up to. His car wasn't among those parked at Nick's. The neon Saloon sign above the door sputtered and blinked as Wayne entered the dimly lit room.

Three day-shift miners were at the pool table and two others leaned against the bar. A pair of soldiers in disheveled uniforms, probably from the supply depot, Wayne thought, and a little out of place in Dragger, sat at a table in the far corner. The usual haze of tobacco smoke filled the place. The wail of a country song blared from the juke box. The miners watched Wayne closely as he walked along the bar to Nick's office.

Nick Zulakis, fleshy, middle-aged, with watchful, deep-set eyes, sat slumped behind an oak desk that nearly filled the small room. His large, round head, its thick, black hair slicked back in an oily pompadour, dominated his short, pudgy body. A cigarette dangled from the corner of his mouth.

"Well, well, what can I do for the undersheriff tonight?" Nick asked, hardly looking up from his desk.

"I doubt there's much," Wayne replied, noting the attitude, "unless you've run into a kid named Billy Preston."

"Why would I know him?" Nick looked annoyed.

"No reason, I guess. He's not in the black market as far as I know."

"That's uncalled for, Wayne. I ain't doing that anymore and you know it."

"Tell you what, Nick." Wayne leaned forward propping a foot on the edge of a chair, his large frame filling the room as he loomed over the smaller man. "I might be more inclined to believe that if you were a little more cooperative. When I ask you about someone out in this end of the county, I expect a better answer." He allowed a humorless grin and added, "looks to me like Jim Wells is gonna have to start coming by here more often to give Curly some support." He turned to leave then looked back. "By the way, Nick, I know Curly brings a lot of his problems on himself, but that's no call to take advantage of him."

Wayne retraced his path along the bar. He noticed the soldiers' drunken giggles while they tried to light each others' cigarettes. He turned to the bartender, "No more for them soldier boys, Curtis."

"Right Wayne, whatever you say."

"Heil Hitler!"

Wayne spun around instantly, catching one of the younger miners by the pool table with his arm still half extended, mouth open in a half-grin and fear beginning to cloud his eyes.

In the same motion, Wayne strode to the pool table, reached across, seized the man by his shirt collar, jerked him up and over the table and sent him sprawling on the floor. As the miner got to his hands and knees, Wayne walked over, grabbed him by the back of the belt, picked him up and carried him out the door. He continued across the parking lot, his baggage clawing and kicking the gravel. The lot ended at a steep slope that descended about forty feet to the creek bed. Here, Wayne stopped, raised the miner to a forward leaning position, grabbed his hair, pulled his head back next to his own and said softly, "The next time you get a notion to make rude remarks to someone's back, remember this."

He pitched the man forward in an arcing somersault, his backside slamming against the ground about halfway down the rough, weedy slope like some large, felled bird. He tumbled and rolled to a dusty stop next to some willows by the creek.

The other patrons had clustered just outside the saloon door, and as Wayne walked past to his car, they shrank back inside. Driving away, he saw two of the miners re-emerge and in hopping, tentative steps, start toward the slope.

Heading back to Collier, Wayne wondered about the two soldiers. He wished he'd got their names. He'd remember their faces. Nick, he thought, should get the message as far as Curly was concerned but Wayne knew he wasn't done with him. And he wondered too, if this little shake-up would bring forth any information about Billy Preston. Time would tell. He noticed Curly's car parked in front of the Dragger Café as he drove past, but he was too tired to stop. He'd be back soon. He expected things to start happening.

Chapter 22

The first thing was a phone call from Curly the next day telling Wayne that Billy Preston had been seen in Dragger within the past twenty-four hours.

"That's right, Wayne, he was spotted by Nick's day bartender down in the creek below the saloon," Curly reported on the phone. "Turns out, he's been seen around there several times in the last couple of weeks. He even came into the saloon once and asked if he could do something to earn a couple of bucks." Curly paused to let the news sink in but there was no response. "Anyhow, Tom, he's the day man, turned him away 'cause he seemed a little young, figured him to be a runaway or kid hobo or something."

"That's real interesting, Curly," Wayne said. "Tell you what, without making too big a fuss about it, see if you can spot that kid and if you do, we'll bring him in. But Curly," Wayne's voice took on a stern tone, "don't try to do it by yourself. You call Jim Wells or me to help you. You got that?"

"Right Wayne, whatever you say. What charge, murder?"

"No, let's keep that under our hats for a while longer. We'll figure the charge after we find him. Any questions?" None being voiced, Wayne added, "Then you be careful, Curly, you hear?"

The next thing was a call from Mrs. Mooney to report that they had discovered something missing that belonged to her father.

"It's a leather pouch that was full of old coins," she told Wayne. "He kept it on a string around his neck."

"That seems a little odd," Wayne replied. "What kind of coins?"

"Real old ones he'd had as long as I can remember," she said, her voice quavering.

Wayne took down a description of the pouch and her mention that among the coins was one twenty-dollar gold piece. He told her he'd stop by to see

74

her that afternoon. He called Doc Clary to ask if such a pouch had turned up among the old man's personal effects.

"Nope," Doc replied, "but that might explain the mark on his neck."

Mrs. Mooney looked tired and even more depressed than before when she answered Wayne's knock and invited him in. "I had forgotten all about those coins," she told him over coffee. "But my husband remembered. I'm afraid he thinks that someone who handled his body might have found them and kept them." She offered an apologetic smile. "He'd looked at them and figured at least some of them were valuable, especially the gold one, he called it a double eagle."

"Well, Mrs. Mooney," Wayne replied, "I checked with the coroner and the officers who were out here that day. None of them saw the coins or the pouch they were in." Wayne finished his coffee and picked up his hat. "It looks to me like whoever killed him could have taken the coins, which offers us a motive for what happened."

"It, it, none of it makes any sense at all to me," she said, tears welling up in her eyes.

"No ma'am," Wayne replied softly, resisting an urge to reach out and offer a comforting touch, "it's a strange situation and I'll have to ask you again not to talk about this to anyone."

Chapter 23

Walking to his car, Wayne noticed a black Chevrolet parked in the driveway of the house next door. Someone, a woman he thought from her size and movements, was working in the back yard. He walked over and introduced himself, showing his badge and touching the brim of his hat.

"Oh, my goodness," said the thin, middle-aged woman looking up from her garden and rising slowly to her feet. She was dressed in a pair of baggy men's overalls, a long-sleeved shirt and gloves. The wide-brimmed straw hat she wore gave her long, pale face a gaunt look with its halo of straw and dark hair.

Wayne offered a smile. "Wonder if I could ask you a couple of questions, ma'am?"

"Well, I doubt I could be much help. I just got back from a trip last night." She gestured at the garden. "That's why this is such a mess." An expression of disgust crossed her face. "My husband's been staying at the boarding house at the mine so he wouldn't have to cook while I was gone. He was supposed to come by and look after things but you can see how that went."

"I'll try to be quick so you can get back to your garden," Wayne said. "I believe your neighbor said your name was Dubois. Is that right?"

"Yes."

"Did you know that Mr. O'Ryan next door there died last week?" Wayne asked matter-of-factly, hooking a thumb toward the Mooney's house.

"No, I didn't!" she replied, obviously surprised, bringing her hand to her cheek. "How, what happened?"

"Well," Wayne said softly, "it looks like he choked to death on something."

"My goodness! That must have been hard on the family."

"Yes ma'am, I believe it has been, though he was getting up in years."

"So he was," she replied grimly. "I'm afraid you won't find much sympathy for him here."

"And why is that?" Wayne asked, a little surprised at both the words and her expression.

"I'm not sure I should be talking about this. My husband and I had decided to handle it ourselves." The grim expression continued while Mrs. Dubois studied her gloves. "If that old fool had died six months ago he'd a saved everyone a lot of trouble and heartache."

Wayne shifted his feet and looked directly at Mrs. Dubois. "I think you'd better tell me what you mean by that," he said softly but firmly.

She looked down then to one side before returning Wayne's look. "He, uh, well, our little niece was staying here with us for a while and he, the old man, got some kind of notion about her and did something bad." She looked away again, as if the words pained her.

"What did he do?" A sense of dread rose in Wayne's mind. He didn't like the direction this was heading.

"He just tried to fool around with her!" She said with some vehemence. "He got her to come in the house and then tried to get in her clothes and touch her." Mrs. Dubois' eyes began to tear. "Gave her a real bad scare."

"I see," Wayne lowered his eyes and reached in his pocket for a notebook. He hated this; this most embarrassing of crimes. It gave him an inexplicable sense of guilt. That any man would stoop to such behavior seemed a stain on the whole sex somehow. He clenched his jaw and went on. "What you describe, Mrs. Dubois, is a pretty serious crime. Why didn't you report it when it happened?"

"To who, that fool of a constable we have here?" she asked angrily. "We thought that would just make things worse for her. My husband had a talk with the Mooneys. There was a terrible row. Then we decided to send Michelene, that's her name, back to her parents. I went with her on the train all the way to Montreal." She paused a moment. "No easy trip these days, I can tell you."

"Yes ma'am. Michelene is your niece's name?" His mind went back to the letter.

"Yes, poor thing," Mrs. Dubois said, her anger subsiding a little. "She'd lived through the war in France and finally they were able to get her out and over here and this had to happen." She dabbed at her eyes with a handkerchief.

"Didn't you just say her parents were in Montreal?"

"Oh, well, to everyone's surprise, they managed to immigrate to Canada not long after they got her out. We planned to let her stay on here until school was over, but when this happened we decided to get her back to them right away."

Wayne nodded sympathetically while Mrs. Dubois talked, rapidly scribbling notes. "Since your niece is out of the country now and Mr. O'Ryan is dead," he said shaking his head, still deeply galled and frowning, "it don't look like there's much to be done about this legally, but I'll look into it just to be sure."

His first impulse was to go back and ask Mrs. Mooney why she hadn't told him about the incident with Michelene. He considered it as he walked back to his car and decided he would return tomorrow or the next day and talk with her then. How much grief, He wondered, could that poor woman stand?

Chapter 24

With the news that Mr. O'Ryan had been murdered, Alan's interest in the matter, sparked in part by fear of being implicated, returned with increased excitement. Now he felt it was time to bring Two-Gun up to date on the subject—with the requisite code of secrecy.

"I would'a told you sooner but I didn't want to make a big deal out of it," Alan explained when they met in the park. "I coulda handled it myself if that'd been all there was to it, but now its murder included!"

Alan described the incident in the willows with Billy and Ralph in a manner that omitted any account of distress on his part and mentioned Michelene's letter without explanation. He went on to theorize that Billy was the logical suspect for the old man's death. "So I think we should try to find Billy 'cause I bet he did it."

"What about the r-reward?" asked Two-Gun.

"Well, you know there's gonna be a reward for a murder case. Don't worry, I'll find out what it is."

Alan wasn't so sure of his facts this time. He had no idea if there was a reward involved. In fact, there probably wasn't one, but he needed Two-Gun's help.

Meanwhile, the object of so much speculation, Billy Preston, was making plans of his own in his new hideaway, a collapsed shepherd's hut in the desert north of town. The dank, sour-smelling interior was dark but for shafts of dusty sunlight that filtered through the holes and cracks in the jumble of propped up rotting logs and planks; all that remained of the abandoned shelter. Billy picked through a bag of food Ralph had just brought.

"I gotta get home to Kentucky, Ralphy. That's the only way I'll stay outta jail." Billy bit into a Baby Ruth candy bar, a scarcity. "My pa can sign me into the army and I can put all this crap behind me." He looked at Ralph through narrowed eyes, smirking at the expression on his cousin's face. "You can quit worryin' soon as I'm outta here. I'll never say nothin' to nobody, but you gotta help."

"You got the money," Ralph responded. "What else do you need?"

"Real money, you dope!" Billy frowned, his words fragmented by his chewing. "I gotta get a bus or something outta here. Them old coins ain't even spendable. The cops'll be looking for 'em."

Ralph stared at his cousin. "I ain't got any. I get fifty cents a week allowance and Dad makes me tell him how I spend every cent. He paused, anxiety clouding his face. "Let me have a look at that dagger of yours," Ralph said, reaching for the knife Billy usually wore in a scabbard on his belt, now laying on a dirt shelf. "It might be worth …"

"NO!" Billy screamed, leaping to his feet shoving Ralph to the floor, holding the unsheathed knife at Ralph's nose. "You touch this knife and I'll gut you like a hog!"

"Billy! No, I'm sorry," Ralph cried. "I didn't mean nothin', don't hurt me!"

A small, one-side smile and stare settled on Billy's puffy features. "I ain't gonna hurt you, Ralphy. You just gotta remember the rule and that is nobody but me touches this knife."

"Yeah, okay, I got it. Who cares?"

Billy settled back into the seat he had fashioned in the corner of the lean-to. "You heard anymore about what the cops are doin' about Papa's murder?"

"It wasn't a murder," Ralph said heatedly. "That was an Accident, and if anyone ever asks all we gotta do is tell the truth."

"Yeah, well, you're really stupid if you think the cops are gonna believe you." Billy smirked, enjoying his cousin's discomfort. "They're gonna put you in jail when they figure out where that letter really came from."

"But you're the one who took his money!" Ralph whined.

Chapter 25

A flat tire on his bike forced Alan to walk to the library. He was anxious to see if the newspaper had any information about Mr. O'Ryan's death. Shirley wasn't there, again. He hadn't seen her for the past two weeks. Checking her house, he surmised that the family was away on vacation. He missed her and their talks. He worried that she might have heard about the sheriff coming to see him. A hollow pain settled in his stomach when he thought how she might feel if he were to be accused of being involved in a murder.

The only thing in the paper was the standard obituary. It reported that Mr. Cornelius O'Ryan, age 76, had passed away, apparently of complications from respiratory disease, and listed his local survivors.

Alan was both relieved and disappointed. No mention of murder, the very thought of which caused him fits of worry. On the other hand, he had hoped to find something about the investigation. There had been no word since the Undersheriff's visit, and his curiosity and imagination were eating away at him. He had just walked out the library door when Shirley rode up on her bike.

"Alan! I'm so glad you're here," she called to him as she came to a stop and dismounted.

"Hi, where've you been?" he asked, his spirits soaring at the sight of her.

"I told you we were going to Denver on vacation," she said with some pique. "Don't you remember?"

"Oh, yeah." He had no recollection of it at all.

Shirley motioned for him to follow her a few feet from the library gate to a large cottonwood tree where they would be out of sight of the building. "Alan, what have you got yourself into?" she asked, obviously upset.

"What, what do you mean?"

"Mrs. Mooney told my mother that the sheriff was talking to you about Mr. O'Ryan being murdered!" Her eyes widened as she spoke.

Alan's heart sank as the words poured out. His worst fears had materialized. "Did she say murdered? How'd she know that?"

"And Ralph told me he thought you and Two-Gun had stolen his money!" Shirley was nearly in tears.

Alan was stunned. Why would Mrs. Mooney say that? But worse, why was Ralph saying such things? Alan hadn't heard anything about missing money. And why was Shirley talking to Ralph? The happiness he'd felt on seeing Shirley now crumbled. Everything had gone wrong.

"Well, did you?" she demanded, the tears visible. "Why did Ralph say that about you?"

Frustration overcame him and he succumbed to a sudden rage. "Ralph! Ralph!" he yelled at her, his face revealing his fury. "Why were you talking to him? Ralph's the biggest liar in town, everybody knows that!"

She fell back, eyes wide, her hands flying to her face. "Maybe he was right," she cried. Tears streaming down her cheeks, she fled to her bike.

Alan, struggling to regain control of his temper as she rode away, reached feebly in her direction and said, "Wait, I'm sorry ..." but she had already gone.

Could things get any worse? Alan felt very alone in his plight. It came to him that he might really be suspected of having something to do with the old man's death. He had talked with him shortly before he died. He and Ralph hated each other, and Ralph would say anything to cause him trouble.

Now he'd made Shirley leave and he didn't know if he could ever make things right between them. He was overcome with self-pity and wanted nothing more than to see his grandmother. He considered running away and trying to make his way back to her farm in east Texas. Surely he'd be welcome and safe there. He had barely begun to think how he could cross those mostly empty miles when Two-Gun rode up on his bike.

"Th-thought I'd find ya here," Two-Gun said, breathing heavily.

"Hi," Alan replied glumly.

"W-well, is there a r-r-reward?" Two-Gun asked, wide-eyed, brows arched.

"I don't know, Two-Gun," Alan spoke in a voice so low he could barely be heard.

"Wh-what's the m-matter with you?"

"I think we may be in big trouble," Alan said, still so perplexed he could feel tears beginning to form. He walked to a fallen tree trunk next to some cedars and sat down. Two-Gun followed. Slowly, Alan regained control of his emotions and began telling Two-Gun what Shirley had just told him. "And I couldn't find nothin' about any reward for Billy." He stared at the ground for a moment. "I don't even know for sure what they want him for, but I still think he had something to do with that old man dying."

"Well, I got some n-news for you," Two-Gun said earnestly. "I found out where B-Billy's hidin' now."

"Oh yeah?" Alan's spirits jumped a bit. "Where?"

"Y-you know that old shepherd's cabin that's all c-caved in out past the dump?" Two-Gun's eyes grew rounder as he spoke. "Well, I f-followed Ralph out there this morning. Looked like he was t-takin' a bag of somethin' to Billy. He's probably still there."

"Did you see Billy?" Alan was fully alert now. If they could get Billy to the sheriff it might solve their problem. He was convinced the truth would come out.

"W-well, no, I couldn't get that c-close without them seein' me. But why else would R-Ralph go there? He never goes out to the cedars."

"Let's go scout it out. If he's there I'll get my mom to call the sheriff. Or we could tell Curly."

They headed out toward the road and turned up the hill toward C Section. Approaching the driveway to Nick's Saloon, they spotted Curly Mayo's car pulling out. Both boys were walking, Two-Gun pushing his bike, and both kept their eyes down. It was too soon to get Curly involved, if he was to be involved at all. But the constable's car had just passed them when it turned around in the road and pulled up beside them.

"Hey, boys, Alan Steger, that you?" Curly shouted, peering out the car window. "I thought so," Curly said, slurring his words a little. "Come 'ere, I ain't seen you for a while. You been staying outta trouble like I tol' ya?"

"Yessir," Alan replied, looking at the ground hoping Curly would leave soon.

Curly's gaze shifted to Two-Gun. "You're the kid they call Two-Gun ain't ya'?" Curly, receiving no reply, changed his approach taking on a more businesslike tone. "Lissen boys, I'm still lookin' for Billy Preston an' if either one of you's seen 'im, you got a duty to tell me. Now, how 'bout it?"

The boys exchanged glances. Two-Gun looked back at the constable. "I k-know where he's at."

Alan cringed and bit his lip. He'd hoped to get the sheriff to handle this if Billy was really there.

Curly stared at Two-Gun for a moment, his eyes bulging. "Where? Tell me right now!"

"H-he's out in the c-cedars at the old shepherd's cabin," Two-Gun replied.

"Where th' hell's that?" Curly was not one to venture much beyond the town limits.

"It's an old caved-in shack out past the dump a ways," Alan volunteered, deciding this might as well be the time to act.

"Show me the way out there!" Curly demanded, popping his head out the car window, knocking his hat askew.

Chapter 26

A low screen of dust kicked up behind Curly's old Ford as it turned out of C Section onto the dirt road to the town dump following Two-Gun on his bike. Alan rode in the car. The little procession came to the dump entrance which was heralded by a bullet-pocked wood sign proclaiming the Dragger Sanitary Disposal.

The dump sat in a gully a couple of hundred feet further into the cedar forest. From it rose a thick spiral of gray smoke with its usual stench. Here, Two-Gun turned off the dirt road onto a long-abandoned wagon trail, the ruts of which were overgrown and treacherous. As the car bounced and bottomed on the crude tracks, Curly cursed.

"Son of a bitch!" he exclaimed. "Damn, oil pan! How much farther?" He tipped back his hat to wipe his sweaty brow on his sleeve.

"Not far," Alan replied, a little worried about Curly's ranting.

Two-Gun stopped in front of them, looked back at the car and, waving his arms, pointed off to his right. Following Two-Gun's signals, Alan spotted Ralph, partially concealed behind a stand of sagebrush.

"There's Ralph!" he shouted at Curly.

"Where? Where? I don't see ..." Curly stopped the car and got out for a better look. Alan jumped out too.

"There, there!" Both Alan and Two-Gun were pointing and shouting.

Ralph, who had been gazing at them curiously, abruptly took off running through the brush and scrub toward town.

"Stop!" Curly shouted. "Stop there, I say! Name of the law, stop!" Drawing his revolver, he fired a shot in the air. The sound exploded across the desert plain, reverberating off rocks and gully walls, sending a covey of quail fluttering aloft. Alan and Two-Gun were momentarily stunned into round-eyed silence. Curly, too, seemed a little surprised. It took a minute for everyone to compose themselves.

Two-Gun spoke first. "Th-there's the shack where Billy's at," he said, laying his bike on the ground and pointing up the trail at what appeared to be just a rough mound of dirt.

"I don't see nothin'," Curly said, peering in that direction. "Where you say?"

"There, that mound yonder," Alan said starting toward it. "The shack's caved in. He's dug in under a lean-to on the other side."

"You wait a minute," Curly said loudly and soberly. "You both wait here by the car. I'll look for Billy." Curly holstered his gun, adjusted his hat and walked a little unsteadily toward the mound. Alan and Two-Gun trailed a short distance behind him.

Nearing the mound, they saw the logs and boards collapsed over a primitive rock foundation. A shadowed opening at one end appeared to be the entrance. Curly leaned down, squinting into the gloom.

"Billy! Billy Preston! You in there? This is Curly Monroe, the constable. Come on out here!"

No reply.

Curly moved a little closer. "Don't make me have to come in there after you, Billy!"

Again drawing his revolver, Curly bent over and entered the cave-like darkness. Alan and Two-Gun, watching as Curly disappeared into the mound, waited, their breathing almost suspended.

"OOOH-AARGH!" Curly's voice. "Ahhh, son of a bitch!" He reappeared, coming out of the mound clutching his side.

Alan had never seen Curly without his hat and the whiteness of his bald pate was the first thing he noticed.

"He stuck me!" Curly loped toward the car. Blood matted on the right side of his shirt and his hand with which he was covering the wound. "Git in th' car! Git in th' car!" he yelled at the boys, swinging his free hand at them. Curly hurled himself into the driver's seat. "Gotta get help! Hurry, git in here!"

Alan and Two-Gun clambered in through the passenger door.

Curly's face and head gleamed with perspiration as he started the car and set off in a wide circle through the dirt and brush, the wheels spinning and kicking up clouds of dust. But Curly misjudged his distance and instead of returning to the trail the car veered into the edge of a shallow dry wash coming to a halt next to a stand of cedar and tall sage. The wheels spun uselessly as the car tilted to one side buried up to its axle in soft sand.

Curly's head flopped back, then his chin dropped to his chest. Was he dead? What if he was dead all because he and Two-Gun got him to come out here after Billy? The boys scrambled out, barely able to push their door open against the brush, and scurried around to the driver's door, jerking it open.

Curly looked at Alan. "Get help."

"Two-Gun!" Alan shouted. "Ride to the fire station and tell 'em what's happened and where we are!"

Two-Gun stood frozen, mouth agape.

"Go on! I'll stay here with Curly, he may be hurt bad."

"Ah, ah, okay!" Two-Gun responded, running to his bike and pedaling away toward town as fast as the sandy terrain allowed.

Alan turned his attention to Curly, who raised his head and looked at him.

Fumbling, Curly took the keys from the ignition and handed them to Alan. "In th' trunk, first aid box, get some bandages and bring 'em here."

Following Curly's directions, Alan fashioned a compress from the cloth and pressed it against the wound. Using another length of cloth, he stretched it around Curly's torso and tied it tightly over the compress.

Curly slumped down in the seat. "I'll just rest a minute," he said, closing his eyes.

"Is he dead?" Billy's voice behind him.

Alan jumped back from the car, startled, a cold chill suddenly climbing his back making his scalp tingle and crawl. Billy stood about ten feet away, Curly's revolver dangling from his right hand.

"Did he shoot Ralphy?"

Finding his voice, Alan stared at Billy a moment before speaking: "No, no he ain't dead and he didn't shoot Ralph. Ralph's probably home by now."

Billy took a step forward.

"Stop!" Alan barked. "Don't come no closer!"

Billy stopped, a slight grin and look of recognition on his face. "Well, if it ain't the purty boy. What're you doin' here? So you're the one that's got the cop out here. You ain't only a sissy boy, you're a squealer too."

"You just go over to that rock yonder and sit down!" Alan said with as much authority as he could muster. "The sheriff's on his way out here right now. He'll probably be here any minute."

Billy waggled the pistol, leveling it in Alan's direction. "You ain't in no spot to be givin' orders to nobody," he said, narrowing his eyes. "Tell ya what, purty boy, you're gonna help me out here and if you do good, I might let you go. How's that sound?"

Alan stared at the gun, his mouth very dry. "You, you better just put that down and go sit on that rock there," he said again, trying to control a rising panic. "The sheriff's coming!"

Billy grinned. "Yeah, well he better hurry 'cause you 'n that constable ain't gonna be around when he gets here." Billy took a couple of short steps toward the car. "Here's what's gonna happen, purty boy. You're gonna reach in and get that feller's billfold, it's probably in his back pocket, and you're gonna give it to me, see?

"Then what?"

"Why then I'll jest light outta here and you can sit down and wait for that sheriff." Billy waggled the gun again. "Now, jest get it and I'll be on my way."

Alan tried to get his mind around what was happening to him and what Billy wanted. The panic was receding and the weeks of resentment and hatred he had repressed since that dark day in the willows began bubbling forth. Now, Billy was trying to make him a crook too.

Before he even realized what he was doing, Alan slammed the car door shut, causing Curly to slump across the seat on his side with a low moan. Running around to the front of the car, Alan ducked behind the steaming radiator.

Billy fired a round through the open window of the driver's door and out through the windshield, shattering the lower right corner. The pistol recoiled sharply, flying out of Billy's grasp and back over his shoulder. It landed in the dirt a few feet behind him. The look of surprise on Billy's face turned to one of disbelief as he stared at his empty hand. He turned and scrambled back toward the gun.

Alan, shaken by the noise, frantically looked about. He knelt in the rocky bed of the dry wash behind the car. Stones of all sizes lay at his feet. Grabbing a handful as Billy bent to retrieve the gun, Alan waited for him to straighten up then let fly a large, flat rock. It struck Billy's left shoulder blade causing him to yelp in pain. He spun around, the gun gripped in both hands pointed back at the car.

"Okay, purty boy, you wanna play dirty?" Billy peered at the car and the area around it.

Alan scurried to the scrubby brush at the rear of the car where, crouching down, he grabbed more rocks and planned his next move.

"Hey, purty boy!" Billy shouted again. "Here's a game for ya," he said loudly, moving up next to the car and pointing the pistol down through the driver's window. "I'm gonna count to three, and if you don't come out here and get this feller's billfold for me, I'm gonna shoot him and it'll be all your fault."

Billy paused, waiting for a reply, perspiration collecting on his brow. "You'll never sleep at night for the rest of your life knowin' how you caused this poor feller to die like a dog." Another pause. "Okay, I'm gonna count to three! One!

I'm countin' slow so's you can get it through your thick head that you can save this feller. Two!"

Alan stepped from behind the brush no more than five feet from the back of the car, his arm cocked to throw. Billy caught the movement from the corner of his eye, whirled to the right and fired. The sound, again, cannon-loud, was simultaneous with the shattering of the car's side and rear windows, a metallic thunk from the raised trunk lid and an angry zing as the remnant of the bullet passed within inches of Alan's right ear. At the same moment, Alan hurled a smooth, walnut-sized stone.

Billy was, by this time, facing Alan. But with the discharge of the revolver, the attendant recoil and smoke, it's doubtful he saw him. Nor could he have seen, though looking right at it, the rock coming directly toward him. It struck the center of Billy's forehead with a resounding "THWOK," splitting the skin to the bone. Blood gushing down his face, Billy collapsed senseless, sprawled in the dirt.

Alan ran to him, another rock at the ready, wondering if he'd killed Billy. He was seized by the force of competing instincts: a rush of elation and a sense of accomplished revenge made him want to let out a victory yell. And, at the same time, a vague fear stirred him to think he may have gone too far. The need to make sense of this bewildering situation compelled him to calm down and take action.

He ran to the car, where Curly still lay across the seat covered with a scattering of glass shards from the windows. A little moan and small, jerky movements confirmed that he still lived. Alan breathed a quick prayer of thanks and said aloud, "Everything's gonna be okay."

He went back to Billy. Blood still oozed from his head into a spreading puddle seeping into the ground. Alan fretted over the notion that he might have killed Billy. Could he have done murder? Would God and the law punish him? But a close look showed Billy was breathing.

Alan returned to the first aid box in the car trunk for a bandage. He took one back and wrapped it around Billy's lolling head. As he secured the bandage, a sense of mastery came over him. He no longer felt afraid or angry, but almost serene, victorious. He began scanning the trail for signs of help. How long had Two-Gun been gone?

Chapter 27

Wayne had just finished a meeting with Deputy Jim Wells at the Dragger Café and was preparing to leave for Green River when they heard three short bursts from the town's air raid siren.

"Something's up," Deputy Wells said, reaching for his hat. "That's a volunteer call out."

"Let's go see," said Wayne.

They arrived quickly at the firehouse, a cinder-block building large enough for a pair of trucks. Two-Gun, leaning on his bike, was talking to the duty volunteer.

Wayne hurried over to the still panting Two-Gun. "What's all the commotion about?"

Two-Gun looked up at Wayne. "B-Billy Preston st-stabbed Curly Mayo out in the desert!" he said, between breaths. "He may be r-real b-bad off. M-My friend Alan's still out there with him!" Two-Gun took another gulp of air. "B-Billy's out there l-l-loose too!"

A siren could be heard for several minutes before Alan spotted the red Dragger fire truck and Wayne's green Buick lumbering across the desert toward him. Two-Gun stood and waved from the open cab of the truck as it drew near, then jumped down and ran to Alan.

"Y-you okay?" Two-Gun asked, his eyes bulging with excitement.

"Yeah," responded Alan, jubilant at the sight of Two-Gun and the others.

Wayne's car pulled up beside the truck. The big lawman and Deputy Wells climbed out. They went directly to Billy, as did the two fire volunteers. Wayne, noting Billy's condition, went on to Curly's car and motioned the others over. After considerable tugging and pulling they managed to lift Curly out, get him on a stretcher and into the fire truck's open bed. Turning their attention back to Billy, they checked his bandage and loaded him in beside Curly, strapping both down for the rough ride back.

"Jim, you ride back in the truck," Wayne instructed the deputy. "That kid's under arrest and in your custody." Taking a slow, deliberate survey of the scene, Wayne turned to Alan. "You okay, son? Not hurt or anything?"

Alan shook his head vigorously. He felt an overwhelming sense of relief frozen in this moment it seemed he'd survived the day for.

"Okay," Wayne said. "Take a minute to catch your breath then tell me what happened out here."

Alan tried to slow his racing mind. He and Two-Gun gathered next to Wayne's car where the big man stood with one boot resting on the running board supporting his steno pad on his thigh as he took notes. He leaned forward, looking intently at them.

Alan opened his mouth, stammering a bit. The story tumbled out so rapidly that Wayne had to ask him to slow down and repeat himself several times. As Alan slowed and paused, Two-Gun chimed in offering bits that Alan had bypassed. With Wayne moderating, they finally told their tale.

"Well," Wayne said after listening to Alan's somewhat truncated account, "I don't think I've ever seen or heard anything quite like this in my life." He shook his head in astonishment. "It took a lot of nerve to take on someone with a gun like that." Wayne gave Curly's rusty revolver a quick once-over before stowing it in his briefcase.

"Th-there's Billy's hideout," Two-Gun said, pointing to the mound. "I trailed Ralph out here this morning and f-found it."

Wayne followed the boys to the mound. They had to pull away several logs and planks before Wayne could get inside to look around. A quick search revealed a number of food wrappers and comic books scattered about, Curly's battered fedora, Billy's bloodstained knife on the dirt floor and, tucked back in a corner, a small leather pouch containing a half-dozen old coins.

Collecting the hat, knife and pouch, Wayne turned to the boys and said, "Good job, fellas. Let's go."

Bouncing along the trail back toward town in the Buick, the boys crowded together in the front seat beside him, Wayne said, "We're going to the fire station. I'm gonna have you tell your stories to Deputy Wells so he can get a report started then you can both go home." A few minutes of silence passed. "I'm thinking maybe I should go by and see your mothers first and let them know where you're at so they don't get too worried. How'd that be?" Wayne cocked his head toward them.

"Yessir!" they both answered.

During brief stops at the Steger and Oakley homes, Wayne outlined the day's events and the roles Alan and Two-Gun played in them. This elicited the kind of bewildered looks from the boys' mothers and siblings they might display toward aliens from Mars. Both mothers were shocked that their sons, known idlers and shirkers, had suddenly been transformed into heroes. But Wayne spoke convincingly.

Chapter 28

After dropping the boys off at the fire station, Wayne drove directly to the Mooney residence. Mrs. Mooney answered the door.

"Afternoon, Ma'am," Wayne said, removing his hat. "I have a notion you may know why I'm here. Is Ralph home?"

"Yes," she said. She wore a fresh house dress but looked tired. She held the door open. "Come in."

Ralph sat at the kitchen table, a hangdog look on his face. Wayne looked at him without speaking then turned back to Mrs. Mooney. Reaching in his pocket he brought out the leather pouch and held it up for her to see.

"Can you identify this Mrs. Mooney?"

"Oh, my lord," she cried, covering her mouth with her hand. "That was Papa's. Where …" She fell silent.

"We're going to have to keep this for evidence for a while," he said. "It'll be returned to you later."

Turning back toward the kitchen, Wayne put his hat and briefcase down on a chair at the table and pulled out another one. He sat down and faced Ralph.

"Son," he began, speaking very calmly, "I think you have some things to tell me and the best advice I can give you is that you tell the absolute truth." Wayne took a steno pad and pencil from his briefcase and put them on the table. "Now, what happened out there in the desert this morning?"

Ralph fidgeted in his chair and looked up at his mother who stood to one side.

"I should tell you," Wayne said, "that I've already seen Billy."

"Well, sir," Ralph began, "all I know about this morning is that I took some candy and stuff out to Billy." Ralph twisted in his chair. "And on the way back the constable yelled at me and shot his gun off." Tears trickled down Ralph's cheeks. "So I got scared and ran on home."

"All right, that's fine," Wayne said. "Now, let's go back to the day your grandpa died. Do you remember what you did then?"

A long silence as Ralph stared at the table top, squirming in his seat. "Well, uh, sir, no matter what Billy said, what happened was accidental, I swear."

"What did happen?" Wayne asked softly, leaning forward with an inquisitive look.

"Papa, he liked to tease me," Ralph said slowly casting a glance at his mother. "Anyhow, Billy was here that day and him and Papa got a letter of mine and was playing keep-away with it."

"Your cousin Billy, who you saw this morning?"

'Yessir, so Billy wadded it up in a little ball and they was tossin' it back and forth and I was tryin' to get it." Ralph looked at Wayne then back at his mother, both of whom remained silent. "Well, I started getting' mad and when I ran to Papa to try and grab it from him he made one of his big toothless grins and popped it in his mouth like he was gonna eat it." Ralph's head slumped to his chest. He wrung his hands in his lap, "So I grabbed for it and it went down his throat."

"What was that?" Wayne said, leaning closer. "I didn't quite get that."

But Mrs. Mooney had, and she began sobbing, hands over her face. Wayne scribbled in his notebook.

"What happened then," Wayne asked, looking up from his notes.

"I guess he died," Ralph replied. "He kinda tried to grab his throat and then just slouched down in his chair."

"Did you or Billy do anything to try and help him?"

Ralph squirmed some more. "Billy got up next to him and said, 'Well, he's dead' and he told me I'd done murder and would probably get hung."

"What else?"

Ralph wiped his eyes and nose with the back of his hand keeping his head down and, still tending to mumble, said, "Billy seen the pouch hanging from Papa's neck and said 'he won't need this no more' and he grabbed it and gave it a yank that jerked Papa right outta his chair onto the floor."

Mrs. Mooney let out a little gasp and turned away.

"What happened to the pouch and coins, Ralph?" Wayne asked calmly, flipping a page in his notebook.

"Billy kept 'em," Ralph said, his shoulders sagging.

"Okay, Ralph, you're doing just fine," Wayne offered a reassuring smile. "Just one more thing: where did you get that letter?"

Ralph fell silent, staring down at the floor.

"I know where you got it," Wayne looked directly at him. "But I want to hear it from you and I want the truth."

"From Alan Steger, it was his."

Mrs. Mooney followed Wayne to the door, still trying to dry her tears. "We'll bring Ralph in to you whenever you let us know," she assured Wayne.

She had held up pretty well, Wayne thought. The boy's admissions had to hurt. He wondered briefly how he'd feel in that spot. As he put his hat on and turned to say goodbye she looked up at him, eyes dry now, a determined look on her face.

"I can't imagine what you must think of our family, sheriff. We're not bad people. We've got another boy in the army overseas. And what happened to Papa, I just can't understand. After all he'd been through, how could it end like this? He spent his life down in them old mines, crawling on his hands and knees digging coal out of that deep, damp blackness with a pick and shovel." She stopped, swallowed and wiped at her eyes with her hanky. "He worked like a beast of burden just to feed us. I don't know how many times he got hurt, nearly killed in cave-ins. And finally, when he couldn't even breathe from the black lung, the company just cast him out." Tears welled up again as she looked at Wayne, searching his face. "It just don't seem right."

Wayne reached out awkwardly and gently squeezed her arm wanting to pull her to him and hold her, offer some comfort, but he didn't. "No ma'am, it don't. Sometimes there's no accounting for the way things turn out. I try not to judge folks by their misfortunes."

Chapter 29

The next morning, Wayne met Tex for breakfast at Crandall's Diner. They arrived after the crowd but the morning's breakfast odors still hung in the air. After they got seated and placed their orders, Tex gave Wayne a quizzical look.

"Well, are you gonna tell me about the excitement out in Dragger or am I gonna have to read about it in the paper?"

Wayne grinned and said, "Of course I'm gonna tell you. Just let me get some coffee down so I can be clear about it." He took a couple of sips and leaned back in his seat.

"I gotta say, I never saw anything like what those boys pulled off yesterday. I mean that kid put up one hell of a fight. What an arm! He's got a future in baseball if he stays with it."

Tex nodded. "I read Jim Well's report. Hard to believe a kid would have that much gumption."

Wayne took a manila envelope from his coat pocket and opened it. "I was wondering, do you think we oughtta let him have a look at his letter? It is evidence and we'll need it if there's a trial, but, given the circumstances, maybe we could at least let him read it."

The sheriff reached over, took the letter from Wayne and opened and read it. "Well, I don't see how it could hurt to let him see it now," Tex said folding the letter and handing it back. "But like you said, its evidence. We'll give it to him after all this business is settled. How do we stand on the legal part here?"

"First of all, it don't look like we have much of a case for murder of the old man if what I've got is right, maybe manslaughter. It surprised me that the Mooney boy talked so easy but I think he'd held out as long as he could. And the little run-in with Curly scared him." Wayne went on, explaining the details of his interview with Ralph.

Tex looked at him, eyes narrowed. "Are you certain that what he told you was the truth?"

Wayne's face settled into a frown. "He's twelve years old, and you'd have to wonder how good he was at the facts. But I believe that he believes every word he said."

The sheriff looked at Wayne for a long moment and then gave a barely perceptible nod.

"How's the other kid and Curly doing?" Tex asked, genuine concern in his voice.

"Billy's got a skull fracture and concussion; may be a while before he'll be in any shape to question. We've got some serious charges on him but it's hard to say how Judge Morrison will come down on it, the boy being a juvenile and all." Wayne shifted in his seat and grinned. "As for Curly, he's always had more luck than sense. He's gonna pull through and get his appendix out in the bargain."

Word of Billy's arrest spread quickly in Dragger. Alan and Two-Gun were hailed as heroes by most folks, although saving Curly Monroe's life was considered a dubious accomplishment at best. Alan, who normally would have reveled in the attention, was instead trying to sort out his confused emotions as gossip about Ralph's connection with Michelene spread.

All manner of lurid stories erupted and most found their way back to Alan. He felt the noble aspects of the feelings he'd had for Michelene dissolve. He began to feel betrayed. Not by her, or even Ralph, but by his own credulity. It came to him in his misery that both of the girls he'd idealized in his romantic dreams had been soiled by their associations with the despicable Ralph. He blamed himself for being a fool but still burned with jealousy.

Alan settled into a melancholy mood in which he accepted the praise of his peers with a dismissive shrug that, in light of his new reputation, was seen as commendable modesty. The story of his battle with Billy was exaggerated with every telling to where some asked to see his bullet wounds. Two-Gun's role was likewise inflated, putting his ride to the fire house on a par with Paul Revere's.

Ben, meanwhile, basked in his brother's reflected glory and contributed to its enhancement. He marketed used comic books guaranteed to have been read personally by Alan at twice the going rate. And, he would, with proper inducement, reveal interesting, though usually imaginary, personal tidbits about the hero.

Fame played out differently in the Oakley home. While Two-Gun's mother and sisters plied him with attention and pampering previously unknown to him, his father took exception. He complained to pals at Nick's that the boy was getting spoiled. It wasn't long before Two-Gun again felt the sting and wore the marks of his father's razor strop.

Alan hadn't seen Shirley since she ran away from him that morning at the library. He thought of her often, regretfully, unable to disassociate her from Ralph and imagining all manner of distressing connections between them. He wanted to talk to her and clear his mind of those agonies. But he feared she wouldn't see him and what she might say if she did.

One morning, a week after Billy's arrest, Alan went to the library and found Shirley there. She was sitting at one of the tables reading when he walked in. She looked at him with a surprised expression and he immediately lowered his head and walked back to the newspaper shelves. He sat there wondering if he should go talk to her, or if she might come back to him like that first time. Instead, he heard her say something to the librarian then the front door closing. By the time he'd made up his mind to go after her and got outside, she was riding away on her bike.

Alan, afoot, crossed the creek and climbed one of the steep trails through the brush up the hill to C Section. This one brought him out on Grassy Trail Drive a few houses up from Shirley's.

He walked down to it and stopped, staring at her bicycle parked in the driveway. He had been there a couple of minutes when Mrs. McCann came out on the porch with a dust mop and noticed him.

"Can I do something for you?" she asked, shaking the mop.

"Uh, no thank you ma'am," he said, startled.

"Are you a friend of Shirley's? She's in the house if you want me to call her."

Alan didn't know if he was a friend or not and he couldn't think of a reply. He just stood there as though rooted to the spot. Mrs. McCann wagged her head and went back inside.

A short while later, Shirley emerged, "Do you want something, Alan?"

He jammed his hands in his pockets and studied the ground. "I'm sorry for the way I yelled at you," he said.

When he raised his eyes Shirley was standing directly in front of him, smiling. She took his arm and led him into the house.

"I've got something to tell you," she said as if nothing unusual had ever occurred. "Sit down at the table," she directed, like his being there was quite normal. "Would you like some Kool-Aid? I'm just having some myself." She placed a glass in front of him and walked out of the room. He sat there gazing around the tidy kitchen at its fancy curtains and spotless floor. He was wondering how he'd come to be there, when she reappeared holding a piece of paper.

"Guess what?" she said, smiling her bright, beautiful smile at him. "I got another letter from Michelene. Her uncle got her father a job here. She's coming back!"

Chapter 30

Doc Clary walked flat-footed, every step falling with a solid clump, the sound of which announced his arrival much like the lingering traces of pipe smoke marked his departure. He entered the door to the sheriff's office and approached Sadie Mercer's desk.

"Good morning Doctor Clary," she said, smiling.

"And the same to you, my dear; you look very pretty today." He'd never spoken to her without offering a compliment. "Is our sheriff in this morning?"

"No, he's gone to Provo today." She waited for a reply but seeing Doc's countenance fall, added, "Wayne's here."

"Wayne will be just fine."

"Morning, Doc," Wayne said, emerging from his office. "What brings the coroner out this early in the day?"

"Well," Doc said, running his fingers through his bushy hair then reaching out to shake hands, "I wanted to see what you were going to do about the Dragger case, Mr. O'Ryan."

Wayne looked at him a moment. "Oh, yeah, our so-called murder, come on in my office."

Wayne took a folder from his desk drawer. "Tex and I talked with Judge Morrison about this the other day. He doesn't see any point in prosecuting the Mooney boy. We're all satisfied the death was accidental. The other boy, Billy, may be sent back to Kentucky on a probation violation when he recovers. Didn't anyone talk to you?"

"I saw Judge Morrison at the lodge. He said more or less the same thing. I just wanted to make sure with you and Tex before I closed out my case."

Wayne started to put the folder away then noticed the envelope containing the letter that had been removed from Mr. O'Ryan's throat. He took it out and dropped it on his desk. "Guess we won't need this anymore. Think we should return it to its intended owner?"

"Don't see why not," Doc said.

Alan and Two Gun had a scattering of small metal discs from their bicycle brakes spread out on an oily cloth in Alan's back yard. They worked diligently to clean and oil them for re-assembly.

"I heard that F-French girl, M-Michelene, was coming back when school starts," Two Gun said casually.

"Yeah, me too," said Alan, showing interest only in the work at hand.

"You know what they said her and Ralph were d-doin'...."

"I heard all that stuff, Two Gun. You ain't gonna believe all the gossip are you?" Alan said, surprising even himself with his anger.

"Yeah, but Benny Hicks said ..."

"I don't care who said it," Alan replied, still angry. "Everybody's been makin' up all kinds of stuff since Ralph and Billy got caught. Ain't nobody knows what really happened."

"Okay," Two Gun turned back to his work giving Alan a sidelong look. "Don't know what you're so m-mad about, no sk-skin off your nose."

"Yours either."

"Okay."

"Okay."

"Okay, y-yourself."

"You too, just shut up."

"M-make me."

Chapter 31

"Well, Sadie," Wayne said, taking his hat from the rack, ready to leave for the day, "you ever going to make up your mind about having dinner with me?"

"What makes you thing it's not made up?" She got up from her desk, putting away her notebook.

"You never answered my question."

"I did too, I asked you to wait."

"Seems like a long wait to me."

"I don't like to rush into things like that."

"Like what? It's just an invitation to have a meal with me."

"Alright, when?"

"How about right now, tonight?"

"It's only five O'clock."

"Meet me at the New Cardiff in an hour and a half, six-thirty."

"Make it seven."

At seven O'clock, Wayne was standing in front of the New Cardiff. He'd called ahead and reserved his favorite table, usually not necessary. The piano player could be heard warming up inside

Sadie arrived at five past the hour wearing a different, more colorful dress. She'd done something with her hair and looked fresh. "Hello," she said, smiling.

"Hello, you look different, in a nice way, I mean," Wayne said, suddenly nervous.

A hostess showed them to the table. They sat, silent, looking around the room; the nicest restaurant in the county, maybe including several of the adjoining counties. The room boasted white table cloths, potted palms, a dance floor and until the war, a host to welcome patrons. And, until the war, a band had played regularly three nights a week. Now, touring bands played there as available but not this evening.

"I've always enjoyed coming here," Sadie said.

"First place I stayed in Collier," Wayne replied. "I knew then I could adjust to this town."

"Do you miss Phoenix very much?"

"A little, now and then, more some of the people than the city itself."

"Anyone in particular?"

"Not particular in the way I think you mean but I had some good friends there." He paused when the waitress arrived with the menus.

They made small talk, mostly about the office while eating. Finally, Wayne decided it was time. "I guess you know how I came to be here."

"What you mean?"

"I mean why I left the Phoenix police and moved up here."

"There was a lot of talk about you, Wayne. I think everyone has heard something about the problems you left behind in Phoenix. That sort of thing always gets out and always gets blown out of proportion."

"Is that why you've been so reluctant to go out with me? Think it might ruin your reputation?" He leaned toward her, "You can ask me anything you want about my past." He smiled and blushed. "I almost said I have nothing to hide. There's a lot I'd like to hide, but no point in it."

"To answer your question, Wayne, yes, you don't exactly come with knight in shining armor credentials." She dabbed at her mouth with a napkin, keeping her eyes on him. "But, you don't know much about me either."

"Well, why don't we agree to spend a little time finding out about each other?" He offered a reassuring grin. "I'll do my very best to make sure you don't regret it."

Leaving the restaurant, Wayne noticed a poster on a tripod in the lobby. He glanced at it, then stopped and stared.

"Next Week—Singing star Inez Miller with Roberto Saenz at the Piano!" Beneath the banner was a glossy, black and white photograph of the pair. It was Inez all right, and presumably, Roberto—plump, mustachioed with a shiny black pompadour—smiling their best smiles.

"Anything wrong?" Sadie asked, looking back at him.

"Uh, no, just remembered something; let's go."

They parted on good, almost real good, terms far as Wayne was concerned. Sadie had agreed to go out again the following Friday evening and Wayne felt he'd overcome her fears about him, at least for now. Off to a good start, he told himself.

But, his joy over Sadie was almost eclipsed with apprehension about Inez. Was her coming here a coincidence, or had she found out where he was and arranged the booking at the New Cardiff? Anything was possible with Inez, Wayne thought. But he tried to keep his assessment of things reasonably rational. It seemed probable that Inez and Roberto coming to Collier was a coincidence.

She'd explained her line of work to him. She performed wherever her agent could find a booking. She'd worked from El Paso to San Diego with her accompanist (formerly the late Harry Miller) and supper clubs and restaurants like the New Cardiff were typical. His question now was, should he meet with her when she was here? Could he avoid it? Given the past, why would he even consider it? He felt himself slipping into the old confusion over Inez.

Wayne spent the better part of an hour that night once again searching his apartment and car for the long-lost letter. He spent most of the night awake, wondering if Inez had some plan to resume her meddling in his life.

Chapter 32

The next morning at the office, Wayne took the letter from the manila envelope that had held it as evidence the past month, smoothed it and folded it neatly placing it in an ordinary letter-size envelope. He scribbled the name "Alan Steger" on it and stuck it in his inside jacket pocket.

He drove from the sheriff's office to the hospital where he visited Curly Mayo and checked on the condition of Billy Preston. Billy had almost recovered and would soon appear before Judge Morrison where the assault charges Assault charges against him would be heard.

Curly would be released the next day. The stay in an alcohol-free environment, rest and regular nourishment seemed to have had a positive effect on his health and disposition. He looked and sounded like a changed man.

"I tell you, Wayne," Curly said, "when I get out of here things will be very different in my life. I'm gonna quit drinking for good now that I got a head start on it."

"Well, I wish you all the luck in the world, Curly," Wayne said. "Hope you know you'll need it."

Alan was just returning from the library when he saw Wayne's big Buick pull up in front of his house a block away. He ran full speed the rest of the way, arriving at the front door just as his mother was admitting Wayne.

"How you doin' there, young man?" Wayne asked as they went inside.

"Just fine, sir, how're you?"

Mrs. Steger hurried into the kitchen to put on a pot of coffee although Wayne had asked her not to bother. After everyone had settled down in the living room, Wayne told them the purpose of his visit. He looked at Alan.

"Remember the letter you lost last month?" Wayne asked, a smile starting. "Well, I think we've found it."

Alan's eyes lit up and he leaned forward in anticipation.

"Before I give it to you, I'll just say that it turned up among some of Mr. O'Ryan's things after he died. You probably guessed by now that Ralph found it where you and Billy and he had your big fight in the willows. So, that's how it got to Ralph's house and in his grandfather, uh grandfather's things." Wayne slowly took the letter from his coat pocket and handed it over to Alan.

"Well, can't you tell the sheriff 'thank you' Alan?" His mother prompted.

"Uh, yeah, uh yessir, thank you," Alan stammered staring at the envelope with his name scrawled across it.

"Why don't you take it in your room and read it while your mother fixes me a cup of coffee, Alan," Wayne said, "then if you have any questions, I'll try to answer them."

Alan sat down on his bed, carefully removed the letter from the envelope and began reading:

Dear Alan,

I am writing to you from Montreal in Canada. My parents were able to come here from France. Montreal is a large city like my home in France where we speak our own language. I am so happy to be with my parents but I miss my friends in Dragger. I wish you and I could have known each other better. I would rather know you than Ralph who lived next door and was not nice. I learned that you had fought him because of me. You are my hero. I wish I could thank you in person.

My parents say my father might find work in Dragger. If he does, we will go there. If we do I hope you and I can be friends again. Please write to me. Mrs. Mahalik has my address.

Very truly yours, your good friend, Michelene Villiers

A little tingle ran up Alan's back and neck causing his hair to stand up. He read the letter three times before he heard Wayne's voice from the living room and remembered where he was. He folded the letter carefully, replaced it in the envelope, folded it and put it in his pocket.

Chapter 33

The following Friday, Wayne and Tex had a meeting with mine officials that lasted most of the day. Sadie had already gone home by the time they got back to the office. Wayne wondered if she remembered the date they'd made for that evening. He called her from his office.

"Hi, just wanted to make sure you hadn't changed your mind about this evening," Wayne said.

"I didn't Wayne, but you hadn't said anything about it and I wondered if you'd forgot."

"No, sorry, I should have mentioned it. Can I pick you up about six thirty?"

Wayne rushed home to change. He'd managed to put aside some of his anxiety about Inez and her pending arrival in Collier, still, he couldn't get out of his mind a lingering suspicion that she knew he was here. Was she planning to try and regain her influence over him? What if she threatened to cause problems with the sheriff's office here? On the other hand, what could she do? He didn't owe her anything, but his convoluted feelings wore on him, causing distraction and misery.

"That was a pretty good show, I thought," Sadie said, "I like Barbara Stanwyk."

"I liked it too," Wayne replied smiling, "ready for a snack or something?"

"Yes, but let's go by the New Cardiff and just have a drink. They've got a new singer there I'd like to hear."

Did she know? Wayne wondered. He looked at Sadie, no sign of a smirk or suspicion on a face he was finding more beautiful every day.

"I've got to tell you something, Sadie," he said staring first at the sidewalk then into her eyes. "The singer at the New Cardiff is the woman I had all the trouble over in Phoenix."

"I know, Wayne. I knew Inez' name before you arrived here. I guess ... I hope you'll forgive me, I guess I wanted to see what you'd say." Sadie looked at him almost apologetically.

"It's not my place to test your honesty, Wayne. I hope you'll forgive me."

Wayne felt as though the weight of all his worries had just vanished. "You do have a right to find out what I'm like if you care anything about me." He looked at her for a minute. "Do you still want to go hear her sing?"

"Why not?"

They arrived at the New Cardiff early and had a bite of supper. A few minutes later, the hotel manager stepped out on the small stage at one end of the crowded dining room. "Ladies and Gentlemen, the New Cardiff takes great pride in presenting for your entertainment—a pause while the area behind him was illuminated to reveal a grand piano with Roberto sitting at the keyboard—Inez and Roberto!" A brief wait while the scattering of applause died down, then Inez came out, wearing a white evening gown, her hair in an upswept style and, Wayne thought, looking like someone from a movie. She opened with a Johnny Mercer tune and followed with a couple of jazz selections. Not much changed from the act she had when Wayne first met her. He looked at Sadie who seemed to be paying rapt attention to the music, and Inez.

He waited until the first break and turned to Sadie, "ready to go?"

"Wouldn't you like to wait and at least say hello?" Sadie seemed quite serious.

"To tell the truth, Sadie, I had sincerely hoped that I had seen the last of that woman in Phoenix."

"Maybe, but haven't you wondered about her? I don't see how you could go through all you did with her and just walk away. Did you give her a proper goodbye?"

Wayne thought for a minute. The last time he'd spoken to Inez had been on the phone during the investigation. She'd told him what she said to the police. He'd hung up without comment other than to say he'd see her later. "I don't know what a proper goodbye would be in a case like that," he said.

They waited, Sadie showing no inclination to leave, Wayne was about to suggest they go when Inez appeared from a side door and walked over to their table.

"Hello, Wayne," she said with a slight smile and a friendly tone in her voice. In fact, Wayne thought, she seemed quite different from the near monster he'd allowed her to become in his imaginings about their past.

"Uh, hello, Inez, how are you," Wayne replied, clumsily rising to his feet. "It's been a while, kind of a surprise seeing you here."

"Yes, me too," she smiled one of her dazzling smiles and looked at Sadie.

"Oh, Sadie, this is Inez." Wayne felt his face heat up and wondered if he was blushing.

"Glad to meet you, Sadie," Inez said giving her a quick look then turning back to Wayne. "I want you to know, Wayne, that I didn't plan this appearance in order to see you. Our agent booked us here. I have to say though; I knew you were here in Collier, people talk. But I had no intention of looking you up. Didn't you get my letter?"

"Well, uh, yeah, it arrived but I lost it before I could read it."

Inez gave him and incredulous look. "That's a little hard to believe, Wayne, but you don't lie well." She looked at Sadie again. "He is one of those rare honest men, painfully so. If you do find the letter and read it, you'll see that I've re-married," she looked back toward the stage, "to Roberto, and I want to put everything to do with Art Miller behind me and, Wayne, you're part of that past. Goodbye." She turned and walked away.

Wayne and Sadie said good night at her door agreeing to go for a drive and a picnic up in Nine-Mile Canyon the next day. That night he made one last, fruitless search of his car and apartment for the letter.

The End

AUTHOR BIOGRAPHY

Sim Middleton worked as a deputy sheriff and a college instructor in Southern California.. He and his wife live in New Mexico where they enjoy exploring the desert and visiting the mining towns of his youth. He's currently writing a crime novel set in Southern California

978-0-595-45631-4
0-595-45631-6

Printed in the United States
115549LV00005B/1-33/P